Hacking th

What You Can See is What You Get.

By Mike McCulloch

To my son.

Thanks for the fun.

Chapter 1

The green rolling hills of Devnent[1] basked in the mid-summer Sun. Photons rained down, driving the growth of ordered living things. The cosmic demand for disorder was satisfied by heat radiated into space to mess things up there. The cows were blissfully unaware that according to present physics, they live by exporting disorder and speeding universal heat death, but is this gloomy physics, inspired by the behaviour of our machines, completely right? It, and a lot more besides, was about to be ripped apart by a scientist in a cluttered basement.

In this particular basement was a circular structure made out of arrays of gold-plated cubes held together by thin wires. Fret, thin, otherworldly and anxious was there with his son, age six, who we shall call Henryk. Fret was pondering, tinkering, procrastinating. His son sat on the floor nearby building a facsimile out of Lego.

Presently, the activity reached a conclusion, both the machine and the Lego copy were ready, and the man said,

“Shall I do it?”

“Do it, Dad!”

Fret flicked a switch and peered intently through the hoops. The part of the room visible through them subtly changed, almost as if a lens had formed within the hoops, but not quite a lens, in fact another thing entirely in that the property we crudely call ‘space’ had just been deleted for a distance of half a metre behind the loops. Fret now picked up a pole with a net on the

---

[1] In this universe, Devon has a slightly different name.

end, from one of their many excursions to the beach, and pushed it through the loops.

'Dad, the pole is sticking out of mid-air!'

Fret withdrew the pole and net, looked at it, shook his head, burst into tears, and hugged his son, which was quite a difficult thing to do since Henryk was jumping up and down with glee as if propelled by a pneumatic road drill. The man sat down.

"It works! Go get your Mum."

Mum came down to see the effect. She was small, dark haired, and organised. She was understandably sceptical about it but being an engineer and therefore always ready to appreciate utility, she was impressed when she was able to put her hand into the empty space that had opened up to separate the two ends of the pole. She nodded with interest and asked:

"It really is separated. How does it work again?"

"What the loops do is delete the space just behind them so the pole jumps over that gap and reappears beyond it."

"So, it's not an optical illusion?"

"No, it's real in a way that Mach and Einstein would have understood. I'll explain later, but we're going to have some fun with this!"

Chapter 2

Fret was making tuna pie and Mum and Henryk were sat doing homework around the wooden table in the kitchen. As Henryk grumbled away at his sums, Mum looked up from correcting them and was in a positive mood.

"Well, you finally invented something that might help the family!"

Dad looked up from mashing tuna in a bowl with a fork.

"How's it going to help us? I invented it so humanity can go to the stars. You know that."

Mum picked up a wooden spoon and banged it on the table.

"Why can't it do something useful for us! You've finally invented something that works, and you want to give it to the world for free, after they treated you like garbage?"

Henryk looked up and laughed at this. Glad of an excuse to bypass his homework.

"Yeah, garbage!"

"They did not treat me like garbage."

Mum was not to be distracted from her tirade.

"…and they won't thank you for this, as usual, and your family will suffer."

Henryk feigned suffering with a rictus of pain worthy of an Oscar.

"Yeah. We'll suffer Dad."

Dad added peas to the bowl of tuna, mixed them up and covered the mess with cream of tomato soup.

"I make enough from online writing and teaching."

"Not spectacular though, is it?"

"What do you want then?"

Seeing that her point was made, Mum put down the spoon.

"Because of restrictions we haven't had a holiday in five years. Let's go to the Canary Islands!"

"Great!" said Henryk, then in reflection "What're the Canary Islands?"

Dad prided himself on being Henryk's live-in encyclopaedia.

"They're islands west of Africa. Oh, be serious Mummy!"

"I am serious. Can't you delete the space between here and there?"

Fret put the fork down in the soup and appeared to be counting to 100 in his head. Henryk chose that moment to leap away from the homework-covered table shouting 'Holiday!' which did nothing to calm Fret down. Fret rounded on them and stood there for a moment, hampered by a verbal blockage and potatoes on the boil.

"After ten years work, I've managed to project a little fishing net over a space of 50 centimetres. Now you want me to project all of us 2000 miles before the Easter holiday?"

"Why not?"

"Yes, why not! Why don't I just achieve world peace while I'm at it!"

Mum picked up the wooden spoon and waggled it, to make her point.

"For such a creative person you sure have a negative attitude."

Fret looked at Mum and there was a whole history of argument in that look. He took the potatoes off the boil, drained and mashed them, piled them on top of the mix & put the dish in the oven.[2]

"Dad?"

"Yes, Henryk."

---

[2] 180°C for half an hour.

“Are we going to the Canary Islands then?”

“If Mummy wants a holiday, then she shall have a holiday.”

That was that, as far as Mum was concerned and she dropped the wooden spoon and hurried out of the room to buy beach clothes online before Fret could change his mind. Fret grabbed a piece of paper and started the redesign. The portal was going to get a lot bigger.

Chapter 3

It was getting close to Easter and Fret was hard at work on the larger portal aimed at the Canary Islands. Henryk was helping with the building, each gold-plated cube had to be positioned just right in the array so there was a lot of distance and angle measurement with a network of lasers.

It had now dawned on Mum that if she was going to step into this contraption, she would be a lot happier understanding how it worked, so down she came to the cellar to ask.

“So, how does it work then?”

“You never asked for details of my work before.”

“Well, if I’m going to allow your work to transport me 2000 miles through nothingness, I’m entitled to an explanation, but remember I’m an engineer, not a physicist.”

“What do you want, pictures?”, he said with a smile.

“Don’t get cocky! Engineering is what happens when physics is forced to be useful!”

"I know. OK. Can we go back to Ernst Mach and Einstein?"

"Yes, I've heard of them."

"Right, well, Einstein considered this train..."

Henryk perked up at this. He knew all there was to know about trains.

"Was it a Cross Country or a Great Western?"

"Er... a Great Western I suppose."

"Cool."

"And this train is struck by lightning at both ends."

Henryk was impressed by this.

"Is this for real!?"

"No."

“Oh.”

Henryk looked crest-fallen and, afraid he was losing his audience, Fret changed his mind.

“OK. It’s for real!”

“I knew it”, said Henryk.

“So. Bang! The train is struck by lightning at both ends. Let’s image the train is transparent, and there’s a guy in the middle of the train who sees these two strikes, the light coming to him from outside the train.”

“Wait a minute,” said Mum, “How does he see the two strikes? Does he have eyes in the back of his head?”

This question completely floored Fret for a while. No one had ever asked that when he’d studied physics at university. They’d all been too busy writing things down and cramming to have time for anthropogenic questions like that, but, then he rallied. He had been thinking about this for a long time and he really felt he should be on the home straight here.

“OK, but look, that isn’t the point. This is not a question that depends on the particular design of human beings. We imagine there’s an intelligence that can gather information from light completely efficiently, so, yes, he does have eyes in the back of his head.”

“Like Grandma! She said she had eyes there,” said Henryk.

“Yes, indeed. Can I continue?”

“Go ahead!”

“Thank you. If the train has stopped, then our train guy sees the light from both ends at the same time, so he says 'Aha! It's a simultaneous strike,' but, if the train is moving forward then he'll see the front strike first because he's moving towards it. So, he will say "Oh, it's not simultaneous".

"But what if the light travels at different speeds to compensate?"

"Good point, but Einstein said, following the ideas of Mach, that things like absolute time and simultaneity can never be measured, but the speed of light in different directions can be measured and had been by experiments all over the world and it was always the same, so he said 'Why not vary time and simultaneity that we can't test for directly anyway and keep the speed of light constant, as observed'. Einstein said the times of events that occur are dependent on how you are moving - there's no one clock in the cosmos ticking time, everyone has their own time and also by extension everyone has their own space too."

"So how does that enable you to delete the space between here and the Canaries?"

"Imagine we now have a train going forward at light speed."

Henryk was keeping up.

"You mean, like the Enterprise at Warp 1?"

"Yes, like that. The flash from outside the back of the light speed train would never reach our guy so he'd never see the back lightning, The logical conclusion of Machian thinking is that for that fellow, the back lightening does not exist. That Machian attitude led Einstein to relativity. Everyone subsequently forgot that attitude, even Einstein after a few years, and just kept the maths that came from it, but it works and it means that if you can never in principle see a thing, then it doesn't exist for you."

Mum grinned and began to shake her head.

"Look, I'm an engineer, and if you're trying to tell me that the Moon isn't there when I can't see it, you've got another thing coming!"

"It's not whether you're looking or not. It's whether you can possibly see it or not. There is a difference. With my loops here, which are called metamaterials, what I'm doing is bending all the kinds of radiation coming from this area of space behind them away from us, so we can never see that space. That means, from our point of view, that that region of space does not exist, so when we step through the loops we'll appear to jump across that non-existent space to the space beyond."

Mum thought about this for awhile.

"A sort of 'What you can see is what you get?'"

"Yes, that's the idea."

She raised her hands as if to say, "That's enough for now."

"Alright. You've deleted some space. It sounds completely mad, but I was impressed with the fishing rod. The big question is, are you ready to put us through it? It looks a bit bigger, but is it safe?"

"The main problem is that I can't put us directly onto the ground, my accuracy in position is only about 100 metres."

"That's good enough."

"We might be 100 metres up in the air, or under the ground."

"...but you can see through it can't you? Why not just set it up and look through it?"

"Oh, I never thought of that."

Chapter 4

A few days later the family gathered in the cellar to see what would happen when the portal was turned on. It was now a twin circle of gold cubes rising from the floor, about twice as large as it had been. Henryk organised a formal turning-on ceremony, doing a dance he had prepared and then flipped the switch.

As soon as it was turned on, all hell broke loose. An intense light poured out of the portal and a gust of hot wind blasted into the room like the jet from a hot fan oven, knocking Henryk off his feet and a whole stack of papers off a nearby desk, but when the wind slowed down, they all looked through the arch of the portal at the bluest sky they'd ever seen. The papers slowly drifted back to the floor. The dust remained aloft for longer.

“That was awesome', said Henryk from the floor, “it blew me over! Why was there a wind?”

Fret was trying to rearrange the blown papers and put them back into order, coughing from the dust.

“I forgot that the atmospheric pressure in the Canary Islands is higher than here. There's a pressure system called the Azores high, so when we connected that space to this, the excess pressure blew air across the boundary into this room.”

Mum was looking through the bridge now at the blue sky and an oven-warm wind was still blowing.

“So why has it slowed down now?”

“The pressure’s partially equalised now - we have a high pressure basement.”

“It’s warm in here. So where are we going?”

“I’ve arranged it by trial and error so we’re just above a beach on Tenerife called Playa de las Teresitas. Have you packed your swimming trunks?”

Henryk proudly held up his small orange suitcase.

“I have packed a picnic too!”

Henryk loved packing picnics.

“Very good Henryk. Mummy?”

“All packed, but I can’t quite believe where we are going.”

“Well, you’re the one for belief. Are we ready then? I’ll go through first. It’s very early in the morning in Tenerife so we’ll hopefully be unobserved.”

He looked at Henryk and Mum, as if expecting not to see them again.

“Go on then,” said Mum, breaking the moment.

Fret stood before the bridge as if stealing himself for a plunge into a cold pool, then stepped through and appeared to jump into the world beyond. A distorted voice came back to the others,

“I’m alright! You can come through now.”

It was Henryk's turn next, but he was not convinced. Squinting through the portal he could see his dad standing there under a blue sky and almost incandescent with the intense sun, and waving at him, but walking round to the other side the only thing he could see was the dusty cellar and his Mum, deftly putting on a rucksack. Fear is often overcome by understanding, and for those who are so young and haven't had the chance to study physics yet, understanding of this kind is not an option, so his Mum picked him up, as if to hug him, and bravely stepped through the portal and into paradise.

Chapter 5.

The seagull was having a good morning. Already he'd found a couple of sand worms and was feeling pleased with himself. The beach was empty with no humans for miles around. The day was typically warm, and the winter rain was not yet restricting his hunting time. He stood watching the waves lap up onto the pristine white sand, some of which had been imported from a place called Africa, though he wasn't to know that, and cawed happily.

Suddenly a rather angular human stepped out of thin air in front of him. He stumbled back in alarm, and, gathering his wits, he flew off to perch on a nearby white, sun-petrified log to recover his composure. No sooner had he done this and rearranged his feathers than another human carrying a smaller third one also stepped out of thin air causing him to fall off the log backwards. This was extremely embarrassing, and he

hopped indignantly back onto his perch to show that he was still in command of the situation.

Then, the third smaller human that had been carried, dashed at him with an orange box in his hand. That was enough for the poor sea gull, who flew away to find a part of the beach where the laws of physics were more stable.

Meanwhile the three humans were in an extremely good mood. The angular one was dancing round humming to himself, the female was calmly laying a beach mat down for them to sit on and the child was running down the beach looking for more local fauna to terrorise. The two older ones ate some watermelon and looked out to sea.

"I can't believe we're here! It's really Tenerife, in our cellar!" said Mum running her hands over the warm yellow sand.

"Yes, it's like the holodeck on Star Trek, but actually real and not a simulation."

"We should come every week. No more crowded Devnent beaches."

"We can come whenever we want, but I guess soon we'll have to go back through when people start arriving. Our portal is rather obvious."

The portal indeed stood there, a dark oval slightly above the level of the beach, and through it could be clearly seen the distorted outline of a dark, cold, damp English cellar.

"I assume we can get back?"

"I tested it. I've put inanimate objects through, and brought them back, and don't tell Henryk, but I also put Dingo the Hamster through and pulled him back, and he was fine, so yes, we can get back, unless the power fails."

"Well, if the power fails we'll have to get back home by plane, but … we have no passport."

"Ha. Imagine turning up at the airport with no reservation, no passport and asking for a ticket back to Heathrow!"

"You didn't think of that? I think we ought to go back now and next time we'll take a passport with us."

"You think that will help? You know how digitally connected the world is now. Well, you just try, as an English person, turning up in Tenerife with no computer record of how you got there. They'd go mad, we'd end up in the papers as the puzzle of the century!"

Mum got up in some consternation.

"Henryk, we're going back now," she shouted at Henryk who was now at the other end of the beach almost hidden in the shimmering heat haze, building castles and shouting at his dad to help.

"Wait a minute," said Dad, "We've only just got here!"

"I don't want Henryk in the papers..."

Henryk stood for a while, arms on hips and ready to argue, then grudgingly turned and began stomping heavily back as if gravity had just been increased. Just at that moment, from the pathway at the back of the beach came a group of three people, obviously tourists given their colourful clothes and bags. They started walking towards Fret and Mum.

“Oh, blast, that’s done it,” said Fret and started packing.

“We’ll have to get back through quick and close the portal.”

“Get back here now!” shouted Mum at Henryk who’d just discovered something fascinating on the hot sand and had crouched down to peer at it.

Mum dashed off to get him, concluding it would be the only way to ensure his compliance. Meanwhile Fret nervously stood in front of the dark oval of the portal to hide it from the oncoming tourists.

Unfortunately, they had concluded that Fret and Mum were English and were coming over to have a chat.

“Hello!” they said as they approached the portal with a jolly English red rotundity. Luckily the portal was partially edge-on to them, so they did not notice it.

“Hi!” said Fret with a grimace.

“Lovely morning, isn’t it? Why’s it never like this is in Manchester, eh?”

"You should try Dartmoor," said Fret, laughing nervously like someone who was trying to hide a portal. Mum arrived back carrying Henryk, who was getting too big to be carried. "Hello," said Mum as she rushed past and disappeared into the portal.

The three tourists were in a tranquil mood, most of them had hangovers from the barbeque and party on the beach they'd had the night before, so they didn't immediately realise the seriousness of what had just happened, but after a few seconds the conversation had no obvious way to go and one of the men, raised an eyebrow, said,

"Hey! Where's your wife gone?"

"Why, she's just over there, look!" said Fret pointing in the opposite direction to the portal, and as they turned around to look, he too dashed into the portal. The portal was open of course and as the tourists milled around and changed their angle with respect to it, suddenly they could clearly see a dark circle hovering above the beach with a dark English cellar apparently within it.

Then Henryk's face appeared inside the circle and said simply with a wide smile.

"We're aliens. Have to get back to Mars, bye!"

Then the dark circle suddenly disappeared, and the tourists were left looking at each other.

"What the hell was that?", said one of the girls.

"I don't know, but no-one's going to believe us!"

Chapter 6

The family were having dinner after a pleasant day spent visiting Grandma and Grandad without the travel time. They were sat around the kitchen table, the French windows open to let in the warm spring air. Henryk was trying to break away from the table to practice his martial arts and being dragged back repeatedly by his irate Mum. In a period of relative calm, Fret suddenly said,

“Jon Luther!”

Mum pulled Henryk back into his seat again. Slam!

“Stay there! Who?”

“Remember that journalist who actually reported on my work years ago, and then was jailed for whistleblowing large corporations? He’s a hero. We can rescue him!”

Mum thought about this for a while.

“I don’t know. Wouldn’t that be breaking the law?”

“Well, only a few.”

“Just because the big fish can break rules, doesn’t mean you can. Be careful!”

“We have a duty to use the portal for good. They’re never going to catch us because nobody knows it’s possible. What are they going to do? Accuse me of tunnelling through space? They’d be laughed out of court!”

"Just don't do anything to jeopardise Henryk's future alright?"

"Alright!"

A sullen silence settled on the table, Fret nursing the suspicion that his wife would put considerations of Henryk above the survival of the human race and an open civilisation, Mum convinced that Fret was incapable of trusting any authority whatsoever and this may well have led him to invent new physics, but it could well end with something dangerous for the family.

Henryk was convinced that his dad needed his help.

"Dad! Can I come?"

"Alright."

"Fret. What did we just agree!?"

"Look. There's nothing to it. We beam in, tell old Jon to come with us and…"

"…and then what? You'll have a Jon Luther in the house. Is he housetrained? How will you get rid of him without suspicion?"

"Good point. Do they still have smugglers in Devnent?"

"Be serious for a minute!"

Henryk had a better idea.

"Hey, let's take him to Tenerife. It's nice there!"

Both his parents took a few moments to realise what had been said, but then they looked at him with some pride.

“Henryk, of course!” said Fret, “We’ll take him to Tenerife, or somewhere else. Besides Jon’ll know where to go.”

Chapter 7.

Tuning the portal onto a London Prison was trickier than Fret had expected. The calculation required to delete space up to a desired location is difficult and caused an error of a mile for every 200 miles. The error was larger for far-off Tenerife, but that is an island surrounded by water, easy to spot from a distance and approach in increments: a prison in a metropolis is not quite as distinctive.

He placed the portal high over London and identified City Airport first, then slowly aimed south of the Thames. It took days of trial and error but was strangely satisfying: the aim was clear after all. Later in the process the increments had to be done early in the morning since otherwise there'd be observers about, including policemen, who probably wouldn't react well to seeing a portal hovering in the air with a person's

face in it.

The real difficulty was finding Luther's cell out of hundreds. He surprised quite a few prisoners in their pyjamas before he realised that it was best to switch the room lights off at his end. At last, late one night, through a mixture of calculation and trial and error, he located it. There was a faint LED light illuminating the corner of the cell and by finely adjusting, with screws, the position of one of the metamaterials, Fret moved the portal in that direction. The light was bouncing off some very reflective hair.

"Who's there?"

Fret hadn't planned what to say. What do you say to someone when you have no obvious body present to say it with? After a while he managed a mixture of nervous bluster, science, and Star Wars:

"Hello. Er... Don't be alarmed. I'm Fret Boarson. I'm here to rescue you. Do you remember me? I've managed to construct a portal to you using new physics."

Fret knew that Jon had studied physics at university and hoped that the mention of a portal would be reassuring.

"Holy crap! What? Where are you?!"

Maybe not.

Fret decided to step through the portal, concluding rather optimistically that it would be easier for Jon to calm down if he was facing a human being rather than a hovering oval of impossibility. He stepped through.

“What the…! How did you get in here?”

Jon stepped back and fell over the chair he’d been sitting on. This made quite a bang that seemed to stop Fret’s heart, and then all went quiet. Looking over the chair it was clear that Jon was out cold.

“Mr Luther?” said a deep voice outside in the corridor. There were steps.

Fret made a pathetic imitation of Jon’s deeper voice.

“I fell on the floor! No worries!”

The steps stopped, and slowly retreated. Fret then began dragging Jon Luther towards the portal. This was not an easy matter, as Jon was not a small person, and Fret was not a big one.

Chapter 8.

Mum was sleeping, and Henryk was sleeping next to her when Fret returned to the bed. Softly he shook Mum who blearily looked up.

“What time is it?”

“I’ve found Jon Luther, but I need some help.”

“I thought you weren’t ready yet.”

“Well, I was practising and he kind of noticed.”

Mum raised herself on her elbows.

“So?”

“Well, it’s a long story, but he ...well... became unconscious.”

“You knocked him out?”

“No! He fell over his chair and knocked himself out. I need some help lifting him and then some moral support before I wake him up.”

Fret, and Mum, hastily wrapping herself in a night gown, rushed down to the cellar, stepped through the portal to London, and managed somehow to half-lift the floppy form of Jon Luther and carry it, dragging over the floor, towards the portal. Unfortunately, one of the cold floor tiles was loose and Fret’s foot got caught in it, bringing down Jon with a thump that was hugely magnified by the circumstances. There was the sound of running in the hall outside.

“Oh damn! Keep going slowly, we’ll make it,” said Fret.

“Why does he have to be so heavy,” said Mum, “Is prison food so good?”

The door flew open, and the guard was just in time to see Jon Luther disappear into nothing through a hole in the air.

“Whaa…!” he said, pulled out a pistol and started shooting at the portal, then realised he was simply shooting at a wall, and stopped. Nothing of interest was left in the room except Jon’s notepad on the bed.

Back at home, Jon Luther was now blinking on the floor.

“Where the hell…?”

He managed to sit up and look blearily around him.

“What the flying flip is going on!”

“We’ve rescued you!”

Jon looked at them with a look beyond sceptical, and then seemed to resign himself to the fact that he was just going to have to get used to the strange places people forced him to be.

“Just tell me one thing – you’re not from the US government?”

“No,” said Fret placatingly, “We’ve rescued you.”

“Right-o. Here comes the big question: how?”

Fret explained the procedure to Jon and, given the latter's familiarity with physics and basic logic, was able to make quick progress. True to his evidence-based background Jon then asked for a demonstration.

"No problem, I've set up another portal to Brazil. I thought that'd be the best place to send you."

"Hey! Don't I know you? Cosmologist, right?"

"Yes."

"I don't think you appreciate the magnitude of what you have invented here. Talk about digital privacy, you've just eliminated physical privacy!"

Chapter 9

The Sun was going down on the Jarugo beach on Fuereventura, making the water look like molten gold. Just above the water line on the white sand were a family of three, the two boys, big and small, making a dam to keep the waves back, the third, Mum, a little further back, reading a novel with a huge sun hat on. The beach was otherwise deserted since this was far from the tourist areas. Besides Mum, a radio babbled

to itself happily.

“Early this morning, shots were heard around Belmarsh Prison in London. The British government has stated merely that a weapon malfunction occurred. In other news, riots continue in London over the recognition of people as hedgehogs and the Russians have threatened that any further expansion of NATO would lead to nuclear war...”

The boys stopped momentarily in their battle with the sea to listen, and then again started piling on the soft sand. Over the waves there was no sound save that of the sea gulls and all three looked healthy and well-browned by the Sun.

“A wave’s coming Dad,” said Henryk in a panic.

“Quick then. Help me reinforce it!” said Dad.

“We’ll save you Mum!” shouted Henryk, scaring the seagulls half a beach away.

The wave came and hit the dam, and was diverted around it neatly, into a pool dug just behind. Henryk then stood triumphantly in the warm water in the pool twisting his toes as they sank into the warm wet sand and seaweed.

“I’m beat,” said Dad and sat down next to Mum, who looked a bit like a mushroom with her hat on.

“Your phone beeped,” said Mum without moving.

“Oh, look. A message from Jon.”

Met Greenwald, who's gob smacked! Thanx again. Jon.

"Well. All's well that ends well," said Mum.

"It's not over yet!"

"Where next? Tahiti?"

"Mars!"

"Seriously? Won't all the air be sucked out of the cellar if you make a bridge to Mars?"

"Possibly..."

"You don't see that as a problem then?"

"It's a problem yes, but a solvable one."

"How? Besides, I don't want Mars dust on the carpet."

"You needn't worry. I haven't even got a plan yet."

"That makes me feel so much better," she smiled.

They both lapsed back into silence, Fret watching the seagulls patter along the shore line trying to follow the water as it came in and out and grab sand worms at the right time. Suddenly there was the sound of engines, and a beach buggy jumped onto the beach and began zooming along the sand in the opposite direction to them.

"I thought this beach was miles from anywhere."

"It is."

"Not far enough then. We'll have to find another one."

Fret had been thinking about Mars.

"That's it!" said Fret

"What?"

"As I said, we'll portal to Mars..."

"Portal is a verb now?"

"I invented it, so I can verb it if I want. Look, it'll be fun: I'll find out where the Mars rovers are, I'll portal up close to them and leave a banana for them to find! What'll be interesting is if NASA dares to go public with having found a banana on Mars."

Mum sat up at this.

"Look, it's all very well you having fun and inventing everything, but can I please ask that you consider making some more money? I know you don't like money, but we need a new patio! And another thing: we've run out of bananas."

"I don't know how to make money, I never have."

"How about this? What do they call those betting places...?"

"Bookies."

"Right, bookies. You go to them, say you'd like to bet that NASA is going to find a banana on Mars, and you act a bit simple, so they don't suspect anything. It shouldn't be too hard for you."

"Suspect anything? You think they're likely to suspect we can get to Mars?"

"Just a precaution. When NASA finds the banana, you'll get some money for all your efforts!"

"I could buy some more gold, I need some more to extend the portal."

"Gold? Henryk needs shoes for the new school year."

"Is there a bookie near us?"

"Yes."

"I'll look into it."

"You also have to go in, you know?" said Mum with a smile.

The family were far too content to notice that a guy who looked very much like an ornithologist, seemed far more interested in them than the birds.

Chapter 10

It was another typical day at the NASA Curiosity rover's control centre in Pasadena, California. The person responsible for controlling the rover on this particular day was Dr Rowena Anklebaum, who was known to be something of a stickler for The Book. The Book being the Curiosity Rover Utility Manual, Version S (CRUM-S). Her assistant was Chip Ohm, a newbie, just graduated from The University of Wisconsin at Madison with a degree in astrophysics, an unsuccessful sense of humour and awed to be working at NASA: keen to do his bit.

"OK, Chip. Let's scoot the rover round the rock."

"Indeed, let us boulderly go where no man…"

"Very funny…"

"Wait a minute. Let's name the rock first!"

"Not again! You can't name every rock we see."

"It looks a bit like a biscuit tin, doesn't it? Let's call it Biscuit Tin."

"No, that would be silly. You need something with dignity, gravitas."

"I'm going for biscuit tin."

"OK. Write it down on the form and let's go."

"You mean, make tracks?"

Chip Ohm wrote ‘Biscuit Tin rock’ down on the form and then began thinking about the far harder process of actually driving the rover without bumping into anything and writing off a 2.5 billion dollar piece of equipment.

“Steady now. Disengage the brake.”

“Forward and left.”

Slowly the rover circumnavigated the Biscuit Tin. The Martian horizon loomed ahead, much closer than that of Earth, because Mars is smaller, and Chip still had to pinch himself that he was driving on Mars. He’d been using this as a pickup line for the past two weeks and it certainly worked, but the effect didn’t last long. By the time he managed to get women to come back to his place the effect had worn off and they concluded that he may be able to drive on Mars, but he was still a wimp with bad jokes and a whinny voice. Chip gunned the engine, and Rowena winced.

“Steady! Those gears are worth 10 million.”

The Mars soil behind the rock was now appearing and it was disappointingly similar to the other Martian terrain he’d seen. Red dust, scattered with small rocks, most of them more angular than those on Earth because of a lesser degree of wear. The atmosphere was thinner and the wind had less ability to move them around and whittle them smooth.

“Hey, look at that! Looks like a frozen apple!”

Rowena looked up from the thick book of protocols she always carried around and her mouth dropped open.

“What the...?”

Standing on the Martian ground, bold as brass and unapologetic was what looked exactly like a Cox’s Orange Pippin. Chip and Rowena had never heard of that particularly English type of apple, but that is what it was.

“Stop the rover!”

They both looked and stared at the red apple for a while, and then blinked a few times to make sure the links between their eyes and brain were still operating properly.

“It must be one of the hackers upstairs having a joke. Move towards it, see if it follows true perspective.”

Chip moved the rover towards the apple, and it did indeed get bigger in a perfectly realistic manner. The apple’s appearance had changed slightly, it appeared to be freezing up as they watched, but on the side of it there was a label, on which could just be seen a Union Jack with the words ‘First Apple on Mars’. Rowena cursed under her breath.

"It's a joke. Those guys in IT are going down right now!"

She stormed off in search of rough justice while Chip looked forlornly at the apple. It had quite ruined his day. Of course, it wasn't real. Everyone knew there were no apples on Mars and there's no way an apple could get onto Mars. Therefore, he was quite sure that the apple was an image that had somehow been embedded in their video feed as a joke. The space around the apple appeared oddly distorted, as if pixelated, which, to him, confirmed the prank. Little did he know that that small distortion was soon to have cosmic-scale implications.

In disappointment, he engaged the rover's brakes carefully, turned off the display and sadly began updating his resumé.

Chapter 11

Fret had been waiting for a couple of days for NASA to scream and shout about an apple on Mars. He'd scoured the web, looking for any rumours. Nothing. There was a comment about the Curiosity rover being down for maintenance and there was a story in PhysOrg about a fight at the Jet Propulsion Lab which controlled the rovers. Apparently, a female technician had beaten up several male technicians there, and the internet was abuzz with the comedy of it, but nothing about an apple.

He was in the kitchen emptying the dishwasher and gazing out at the garden, whose grass needed cutting. Mum came in with her coffee, sparking a rant from Fret.

"You show people amazing things and the more amazing they are the less they believe them. I should have started smaller, for example, sent salad to Scotland. It's a long time since salad was seen there, but at least it's assumed to be feasible."

His wife looked at him hopefully.

"Have you got the money from that bookie yet?"

"Not yet."

Mum was as pragmatic as ever.

"Are you a millionaire? We need money for that patio. No point hating what you can't do without."

At that point Fret's mobile buzzed. A text had arrived,

Look at Zero Hedge. Jon.

Fret turned on his laptop, always close by, and went straight to the site. The headline made him gasp for air.

An anonymous source in Brazil has released secret NASA cables suggesting that the curiosity rover team was recently fired for frivolity after an apple was seen on Mars. One of the former team has been talking to him.

“Oh no!”

“What?”

“I sense trouble,” said Fret biting his lip, ”Jon knows about the portal and he’s just been talking to the Curiosity team.”

“You know Jon. Will he blab?”

“He’s a whistleblower. Of course he will!”

Fate sometimes, or even often, has a sense of humour. Just at that moment there was a knock on the door. Mum glanced at Fret and went to open it, letting the cold evening air in. There on the doorstep was Chip Ohm, who looked completely out of his element and completely unused to knocking on strange people’s doors but propelled by curiosity.

“Hi. Er, I’m from NASA.”

There was a strangled gurgle from the kitchen.

When Chip confirmed that he was speaking to the right people, he asked to come in and Mum reluctantly agreed. Fret was hiding in the kitchen and pacing up and down, when Mum came in to make some coffee for Chip.

"You can't hide in here for ever."

"Is he one of the NASA Curiosity team?"

"Yes. Talk to him! I don't know what to tell him. You can take the coffee through."

Fret took the coffee and introduced himself to Chip Ohm who, like most Americans, didn't beat about the bush.

"Have you ever dropped fruit on Mars?"

It is an inevitable characteristic of scientists that is endearing but extremely disturbing, if you happen to be one, that it is difficult to lie. In science, to get at the truth you have to force yourself to be brutally honest all the time, or as much as is humanly possible, and because it's often difficult to separate the brain into independent compartments, that tendency spreads into real life as well.

As a result of this, the suppressed tension caused by not wanting to let a complete stranger into perhaps the greatest secret on the planet and the opposing tension of being unable to lie caused a complete mental block in Fret, and the coffee and cup dashed to the floor.

"Sorry. I'll get you another," said Fret as he dashed back into the kitchen.

Chip followed, looking like Christmas had come early.

"Well, I guess that answers my question. Let me help. I'm an astrophysicist. What you apparently have makes NASA look like the first pony express."

"Well, I'm not sure I...."

"Otherwise: sorry, but who knows what I might let slip? I do want my job back."

Chapter 12

It was a windy day in the Valles Marineris on Mars. Wisps of orange dust moved slowly along the red basin floor, eddies forming beautiful von Karman streets and pirouetting around the rocks strewn on the ground. The curiosity rover was idle, its camera still pointing inertly at the apple, which by now had shrunk and was frozen solid.

Suddenly the strip of space between the basement and this location on Mars was deleted and four heads appeared in mid-air, peering through a think glass window. One of the faces looked as if it was about to explode with amazement.

"I don't believe it. I just don't..."

"I've explained how it works."

"Yes, but you'll have to give me some time to grok[3] it. By the way, why do you have this thick glass pane here? Makes it hard to see..."

"You know what the atmospheric pressure differential is between Earth and Mars?"

"Of course, if you connected directly, the air from this room would be sucked out into the atmosphere of Mars right?"

"Yes."

---

[3] Grok: to understand something deeply or intuitively. A concept introduced by Robert A. Heinlein.

"And also," said Mum, "I don't want any Mars dust in this cellar!"

Chip cracked up at this.

"Brilliant! The biggest problem with interplanetary travel is the dust you get in the cellar." He looked around, "Actually, it does look a little dusty in here."

Mum tensed her jaw. Fret gave Chip a quick look and a slight shake of the head, as if to say, 'Don't go there.'

Henryk had been looking particularly carefully.

"Hey Dad. Under the apple it looks green & fuzzy now."

"Oh blast," said Fret, "Don't tell me I've contaminated Mars?"

Chip let out a whoop.

"Yeah! Way to go man. You spread our kind of life to Mars. You broke the mold! Get it? Mold?"

"Maybe it's just a trick of the light."

"Dude. I've been looking at Mars for a few months now and I've never seen anything green on it before. Not at daybreak, noon or twilight."

"What have I done?"

"Relax. That's life. It's supposed to spread."

Chapter 13

Americans obviously eat with their forks only, or at least this one did. The family, plus Chip, were sat around the kitchen table, eating dinner. Chip was on hyper-drive shovelling his potatoes in with almost as much speed as thoughts came tumbling out in the intervals between.

“You know what power your invention gives us? Man, we could go to any exoplanet, find out which ones are habitable and spread the human race through the galaxy! You’ve freed humanity from this gravity ball forever!”

“I’m aware of it, but I want this invention to belong to everyone and not just to America.”

“OK, but we won’t tell the Russians and Chinese, eh?”

“Yes, them too! What’s wrong with the Russians and Chinese?”

“But you can’t be serious! It would upset the balance of power.”

“Surely it’ll maintain it.”

Chip became increasingly sure that the discovery should only be possessed by the US, and Fret was consequently getting more and more depressed. Mum looked at both of them and had an idea.

"Chip! How do you feel about a swim on a tropical island? We usually go there after dinner, digest our meal on the beach and then swim."

"Yeah, that would be beachin'! Get it?"

Chip's puns were pretty lame, but people tended to like the fact that he was at least trying. She smiled in sympathy.

"Well then, let's get our things together and go."

Chip slapped his hand on his forehead.

"But I don't have any swimming trunks."

"Oh, no problem, there's no one around to look," she said, winking at Fret, who looked puzzled for a moment and then caught on.

"Yeah, let's go. To that new beach we found, very peaceful and ...well... remote."

Chapter 14

The waves were typically Pacific, in other words big, long period swell. The vast open spaces of that ocean allow waves to develop over a long time and distance, or fetch, as they follow the wind, so by the time they encounter Caroline Island they are huge and the energy they carry in their motion is such that when they break on the atoll surrounding the lagoon the spray reaches high into the turquoise sky. Within the lagoon, were several patches of land with dense jungles of coconut trees, and some fresh water. There was also a yellow sandy beach sheltered from the worst of the waves and fringed with green palms.

Absolute paradise, but of course, paradise depends also on your state of mind and the man on the beach was not happy. He was leaping up and down, shouting at the top of his voice and behaving as though he was in the process of being attacked by bees. He wasn't bee-stricken, he had merely been marooned on the island by a physicist and an engineer who had decided he needed to be kept quiet for a while. They had also stolen his phone.

On the plus side they had returned half an hour after leaving him, to deposit several bottles of fresh water, three picnics made by Henryk and a note saying 'Sorry. Back soon.' This had not helped his state of mind as much as it should have, and he ended up throwing the whole lot into the Ginger Lily bushes, but eventually exhaustion calmed him down and he fished the food out again.

Later, after his first picnic, which was mainly composed of crisps and bread sticks, he sat and looked in awe as the Sun set behind the lagoon and he started to notice the aroma of the place: a mix between the cool salty air from the sea and the warmer perfumed air from the island. The sand was soft and warm. Not the worst place to be stranded, he thought, but how about snakes...?

Chapter 15

They realised, of course, that they couldn't keep Chip on the island for ever. A few days was the moral limit. They'd already paid him a brief visit to drop him a sun hat and sun cream from a height of 5 metres because Mum was worried that he might get sunburn.

"What's your plan?" said Mum after they'd recovered with a glass of wine that evening.

"I'm going to have to publicise the portal soon. I'll send an email to several scientists around the world simultaneously, but I just want to prove that I can extend the range to another solar system first."

"Why? You've proved it can be done."

"I'd like to be the first to Tau Ceti."

"Tau Ceti?"

"It's the nearest solar system that has an Earth-like planet, 11.9 light years away. Imagine stepping onto an alien world, without a space suit. Well, of course, we don't know if it's that Earth-like, but we'll find out."

"Just keep the house clean! I don't want a Tribble infestation."

The procedure for tuning the portal onto a planet orbiting a far distant star at a speed of about 30,000 kilometers per second was extremely difficult. It had been hard enough for Mars, which also moves in its orbit relative to the Earth, but the Tau Ceti system is

11.9 light years[4] away and the star is also moving relative to the Earth at 19 kilometres per second.

Furthermore, the exact distance is not accurately known so the portal opened up in deep space. Fret tried using a telescope to locate Tau Ceti. Unfortunately, it proved to be a pretty difficult procedure and a day later the portal was still nowhere near any recognisable star system.

Fret decided to enlist Chip's help. He was an astrophysicist and a programmer after all, so back they went to the beach.

Chip was so relieved to see them and so excited to be asked to help that he agreed to forgive them and to a policy of international openness. He spent the next few days in the spare room designing a new way to position the portal by triangulating from pulsars (lighthouse stars) and writing an App running from his phone to do it.

He also downloaded a more recent star map so that he was able to quickly find Tau Ceti by pointing a telescope through the portal, looking at the stars nearby and checking their spectral signatures (the colours of light they emitted) with known stars. One day there it was: the star Tau Ceti, looking slightly orange.

A bit of telescope work showed that the system had six planets, two of which were close enough to the star

---

[4] One light year is about $9.5x10^{15}$ metres. A long way.

that water would be liquid on the surface, but yet far enough away that it wouldn't boil off. This was the famous Goldilocks Zone, neither too warm nor too cold, so they had a choice of two. Chip was exhausted but also as excited as a school boy.

"Uff da! We're actually looking at another Solar system, and I can see all the planets! The Kepler satellite found five planets around this star by looking for the dip in its luminosity as the planet passed in front, but we're the only ones who know there are six. I can't believe I know that and think that it is unimportant compared to what else I know! I should say there's a lot of debris flying around in this system, so maybe there won't be that much life..."

"I want to look too,' said Henryk.

"Yeah, me too," said an equally excited Fret.

"OK, guys. Wait a minute. There are two habitable choices. Do you want a warm or a cold planet?"

"A warm one," said Fret.

"Wuss," said Chip.

"Let's have a closer look at them."

Fret changed the lens on his telescope from a 50 times magnification to a planetary lens, designed for looking at the finite discs of planets, and looked, through the portal, at the inner planet which appeared in the viewfinder to be about the size of a coin held at arm's length. It was an unappealing brown colour and was pockmarked with craters.

Chip had a look as well.

“OK. Told you. There’s a lot of debris in this system, a lot of asteroids floating around, and it looks like this planet has no atmosphere because there are a lot of craters.”

“Why does that mean there’s no atmosphere?” said Mum.

“Have you ever tried to have a good party in a crater?”

There was a deathly silence, so Chip giggled to himself and explained,

“OK. If there’s an atmosphere then asteroids burn up before they hit the ground and also processes like rain and wind erode the craters.”

“It’s dead then. Let’s look at the other planet.”

The telescope was moved to point at the other one, further out. Into the viewscreen came the image of a planet with large polar ice caps and a thick belt of blue and green around its waist. Fret saw it first and then let Chip, Mum and Henryk have a look

“Green!” said Henryk “It’s got plants on it!”

Fret burst out laughing, then so did Chip and everyone grinned at everyone else. Chip collapsed on to a sofa.

"Man, this just beats everything I've ever seen. We just answered the biggest question anyone has ever asked, just now! Life elsewhere!"

"We've got to get closer," said Fret.

"More fine adjustment of the metamaterial array then. I really do need to fully automate that, twiddling those screws is killing my fingers."

Chapter 16

The next few hours were full of frenzied activity as Fret physically adjusted the metamaterial array, Chip checked positions with his App and database and the portal crept in fits and jumps closer to the white-blue-green planet. Presently the planet filled the portal without the use of a telescope and using the telescope they could see seas and lakes, though not any indication of intelligent life.

It was Henryk who heard them first as he was standing next to his dad's mobile phone.

"Dad?"

"Yes."

"There's funny music coming from your phone!"

"Don't be silly, my phone doesn't work in the cellar."

"But it does Dad. You said never to say something is impossible if it does actually happen!"

There are nice moments being a parent, when some of the sensible things you said in the past echo back at you from your children.

"You're exactly right Henryk. OK, let's hear it. Turn it up!"

Harry turned up the volume on the phone and the most bizarre sound came out of it. It was distorted and weak but it was also like nothing they had ever heard, far more complex and more rhythmic than tuneful, almost like something by Jean Michel Jarre, perhaps from the album Zoolook, but more so. It was completely alien and layered in to a mix of quick tunes embed in majestic slow ones.

"Bloody hell!"

"Why has my phone suddenly developed an alien taste in music?"

"Could it be interacting with something on the planet?"

"Holy Dylan!" said Chip, and almost immediately the music stopped and was replaced by what sounded like someone lip diddling at an unhuman rate, and then the music started again, in the same bizarre manner.

"Well, ladies and gentlemen, and hamster, the question of whether there is intelligent life elsewhere in the universe has not only been answered, but we can now also hear them speaking!" said Chip in his most portentous voice.

"Singing," said Henryk.

"If you call it singing. Sounds more like hyperactive dinosaurs groaning in a swamp with a frog chorus."

"You're right Henryk. There's no other explanation, has to be alien, unless someone's just completely reinvented music and has hacked into my phone."

"The simplest explanation is usually the right one," said Chip.

"Quite," said Fret, who was a keen fan of Ockham's razor.

"If they can hack into my phone. What else?"

An ominous silence settled over the room.

Chapter 17

It was late spring in the valley, and the farmer was out tending to the local flora. The rain had been intense of late and there was a thin mist over the valley that was slowly clearing as the day brightened and the orange Sun rose in the purple sky. There had been a recent meteor impact and the crater was still red with the churned soil, but already, even after only a week or so, tendrils of fast-growing red repair creepers were invading the barren space and reclaiming it for the collective. The farmer silently asked the creepers if they'd found any useful minerals there, and they responded that there were traces of what we would call cobalt in the vicinity from the meteor. The farmer sent this information along the usual channels to those responsible for minerals, and those responsible for minerals sent a message back saying that they'd already dealt with 120 meteor strikes that day around the globe, one of which had contained essential platinum, so a little meteor full of cobalt was unlikely to be of interest.

The farmer, who resembled a large white floating ball with arms, decided all was collectively well and moved on to the next field, leaving the air swirling thickly with spores and dust in his wake.

A few moments later a portal appeared in thin air a few metres above the ground, and if anyone had been around to look inside they would have seen four extremely excited faces peering out through thick glass from the darkness.

"Weird colour scheme!" said Chip, "and some of the plants are flying around."

"Yes, that is odd."

"How can a plant fly like that? Buoyancy?"

"If only a biologist could see this," said Mum as a flowering plant drifted past their portal, its roots trailing in the air and absorbing moisture from the mist.

"There are some biologists at our university, but they're usually diving into the sea and I'm not sure how they'd react to this."

Other differences to Earth only dawned on them slowly. Further in the distance, almost too faint to see, were what looked like mountains floating in the sky, mountains without support. This meant something to Fret, partly because of the consequences of new physics [5] and partly because he enjoyed playing minecraft, which allows some rocks to float if their support is taken away, but the others just stood and stared. Before they could discuss the floating mountains, a floating ball with slender tentacles hove into view and stayed there, right in front of the portal.

With a bit of women's intuition, Mum realised it was sentient before the others, and slowly rearranged her hair. Chip and Fret were gaping.

"Hello, what's this then?"

---

[5] Self-propelled nanomaterials. In our universe this possibility is explored in the paper: McCulloch, M.E., Progress in Physics, 16, 2, 73-74. 2020.

"A sentient alien," said Mum.

The three males looked on with mouths hanging open and Mum gently waved a few times. The alien waved one of its tentacles back, slowly.

"Wake me, I'm dreaming," said Chip.

"Looks like he's, she's, it's, curious," said Fret.

"Maybe they don't have boys and girls," said Henryk.

"First contact. What are we supposed to do?" said Chip.

Fret remembered a smiling toothy face from the past.

"I wish Carl Sagan was here. I'll bet he'd wish he was as well. Henryk, can you get my History of Space flight book?"

Chip looked suspicious.

"You're going to read to it? It won't speak English."

"Sagan designed a schematic that could be understood by an alien race and could be used to find out where we are, and it was launched as a plaque on Pioneer 10 and 11."

Henryk dashed over the room and was back with the book so quickly he nearly ran into the glass window over the portal. Quickly Fret found a picture of the Pioneer plaque, and showed the others.

“See these two circles here in the top left? That means the frequency of radiation emitted by hydrogen when it flips its spin.”

“I’m about to flip my spin,” said Chip.

Fret was not to be derailed.

“Hydrogen’s the most common element in nature, so this is a kind of benchmark: the most common form of radiation.”

Chip had seen the picture but hadn’t had it explained.

“I’m getting a bit distracted by the picture of the woman. Do you know it’s not anatomically correct?”

“Yeah, Sagan had to sanitise it to get NASA to accept it.”

“How about these lines?” said Mum.

“The fourteen lines have binary numbers on them defining the frequency of pulsars near the Earth as multiples of that hydrogen frequency and the lengths of the lines tell you how far from the Earth they are. This gives an alien a way to find the Earth. If we show it to them, and they’re intelligent, they’ll know where we are!”

Chip grabbed the book and closed it on Fret’s fingers.

“Ow!”

“Are you nuts? What if they’re aggressive? You don’t give your address to every stranger you meet!”

“OK, we’ll talk about this later, but how do we communicate with this alien then? Hang on a mo.”

Fret dashed over to a nearby table and grabbed his pad and a pencil. After a few moments of scribbling he showed them a passable sketch of the alien.

“Not bad. Didn’t know you could draw.”

Fret then showed it to the alien, who came closer to the portal to have a look. After a few moments the alien withdrew and floated there for a few minutes completely still.

“What’s he doing?’ said Henryk, ‘The dust is moving look!”

Sure enough, the motes of dust, and spores, surrounding the large alien were slowly moving to form a shape that looked very much like a human face.

“Hey, look. He can draw as well,” said Henryk gleefully.

“And he doesn’t need a pencil either!” said Fret.

“*And he doesn’t need a pencil either,*” said a mobile in a gurgling tone.

“What the hell is that?”

“*What the hell is that?*” said the phone.

“They’re trying to communicate?”

“*Communicate. Sagan*,” said the phone.

"I think they're picking up our language as we speak more of it."

"*Speak more*!"

"The more we say the more they're able to figure out what we mean."

"But, how? He's only one exo-octopus. You need a lot of processing power to do that."

"They're doing it. Maybe they're like the borg – all joined up as one mentality."

"*Speak more of things*."

Mum, who was interested in linguistics, spoke up.

"I get it. I think it wants us to speak more about solid things that he can see so they can translate our language into objects and work out what is a noun and what's a verb."

Chapter 18

Henryk was employed to go round the house collecting objects and they took turns to point to the objects and talk about them. The alien stayed silent for all that time, but then just after discussing television, the radio said,

"*Turn on television.*"

So they turned the cellar TV on, and the alien patiently watched that for another half hour while they sat around and Fret went to make some tea. After half an hour it said,

"*More TV channels please.*"

"They're getting polite – watching British TV I suppose," said Chip.

They split the TV screen and let the alien watch four channels. For a wide balance of viewpoints they chose Russia Today, Al-Jazeera, Fox News and Henryk insisted on Children's ITV which was showing Horrid Henryk.

Watching an alien watching TV surprisingly became boring quickly and one by one they went upstairs to bed, Chip to crash on the lounge sofa, still shaking his head.

"That alien is a couch potato."

Fret couldn't sleep with such momentous events going on and snuck back down to watch the process. The alien was still motionless in the same place, or was it a different alien? It was hard to tell.

"Hello," he said.

"Hello," said the alien via the phone "We've now absorbed much data on your culture."

"Good."

"*We foresee imminent danger to you and your kind.*"

"What kind of danger?"

Fret head was still half asleep, but he had made a coffee.

"*You are at a dangerous self-as-God stage that we attained four hundred years ago.*"

"Well, you survived."

"With difficulty. *You may not. We'd like to give you a concept, a meme if you like, that saved us. I will give you a simple English phrase which contains it. All you have to do is spread it virally and globally.*"

"Can't you do it? You hacked my phone..."

"It would not be morally right. It is your world. You should decide whether to do it."

Chapter 19

The news of the alien meme was not received well by everyone. Chip was particularly loud in his objections and was pacing up and down the kitchen. His pale face was even redder than usual.

“You’re not serious! How do you know this meme is benign?”

Fret, sat at the kitchen table, biting his lip.

“I don’t, but it makes sense to me.”

“It sounds like a mind-virus to me.”

“That’s actually what meme means.”

“For cryin’ out loud, Fret!”

“Look. I went through it with them, time after time. They allowed me to see their history. They lost half their population in nuclear wars. Then this meme brought them to a higher level of morality.”

“So does brainwashing!”

“I’ve explained it to you. You can see the point, surely?”

“It’s an awesome idea, I’ll give them that, and it’s been suggested before in a less messianic way. But life’s not a game! It’s not Jumanji!”

“Isn’t it?”

“Who knows?”

"It's only a phrase."

"So was 'workers of the world, unite!"

"Let's do it and see what happens! It'll be an experiment! You know what they say 'All life's an experiment and the more experiments you make the better'."

"Which bozo said that?"

"Emerson – one of yours."

Chip shook his head slowly.

"I think the Amish have a point too."

"What's that?"

"Change is optional!"

"But this offers a solution to all the crazy delusions we've seen recently. It'll end wokeism."

"Well, you're the boss – but may it be on your head."

"Alright. How do you spread a meme globally?"

"We need a hacker, I guess."

"Know any?"

"No, but we could ask Jon Luther. He might know."

Chapter 20

Kaliningrad is an anomaly and a particularly tortured piece of the human mosaic. For a long time it was the royal German city of Königsberg (King's Mountain) and Immanuel Kant lived and thought there, walking across its seven bridges. After the second world war this area of Germany, completely smashed up by British bombs and the understandably revengeful Russians, was absorbed by Russia, repopulated by Russians, and when Russia shrank at the end of the cold war, it remained as a small island of Russianity living in an old German city surrounded by the European Federation. It was becoming renowned as a manufacturer of TVs and as a birth place for cosmonauts.

There is a university there named the Kant Russian University. This was where Brus Elbakyanov lived and worked, the man Luther had recommended as being the best equipped to infect the world with an alien meme. It was also somewhat appropriate given that Kant had once said,

'Two things amaze me.
The swirling stars above me,
and the moral order within me.'

Appropriate for a project that involved taking morality from the stars and applying it to humanity, but there you go. Perhaps it was an accident, but who knows? Nature is sometimes poetic.

Brus Elbakyanov was not poetic. He was a bald, fat, angry man, completely averse to human company with some justification since he'd received a lot of insults for being bald, fat and increasingly angry, and he greeted Fret, Chip and Mum when they entered his crumbling office and introduced themselves in English, with,

"Got damn! Get out!"

Chip was rather more used to dealing with abrasive academic types like this, so he took the lead.

"Dr Elbakyanov. We've come to enlist your help."

The professor feigned sympathy.

"Vell. Good luck with that!"

He pushed them quickly out of the room, slammed the door and locked it.

Fret and Chip looked at each other with glee.

"Portable portal?" said Fret.

"Let's do it," said Chip, and they set to work.

Dr Elbakyanov had gone back to his work. In that moment he was trying to break into a bank in New Zealand and award himself a Christmas present from the New Zealand lottery. He was sending a Trojan Horse in to open up the system and singing a song of his own invention,

"Oh, my little Trojan horse,
slip in through the gate.
Open up the bank,
Brus' pay is very late."

The rhyme comes out far better in the original Russian. Finally, after logging into several other accounts first, to cover himself, he was ready to infect the bank, but suddenly, back in the old real world, the world that he usually tried to transcend, there was a footstep that was far too close. He turned and got the shock of his life, screamed, and fell off his chair, banged his head, and was knocked unconscious.

"So, this is the king of hackers?" said Chip standing over Brus.

Luckily, Mum had taken a First Aid course at work.

"I'll get him some water."

"How's he going to drink water? He's unconscious!"

Mum went to the sink, filled a dirty beaker, and splashed it in Brus's face. He waggled his fleshy chops and said,

"Eto piz-detz!" (a rude exclamation)

He switched to English.

"What hell! You don't look NSA," he said, "How you get through my door?"

He looked at his door in amazement, to confirm it still had the eight locks he had installed on it. Then he looked back at his visitors with a new respect. Chip now tried to explain, with an ironic glance at Fret.

"Dr Elbakyanov, we intend you no harm, but we'd sincerely like you to destroy Western civilisation as we know it."

Brus slowly smiled for the first time in ten years.

"It would be my pleasure!"

Chapter 21

Back at home, the family, Chip and Brus were sat around the kitchen table with some beers (Henryk sat proudly with a ginger beer) revelling in the success of their endeavours. A radio burbled happily to itself:

"There have been strange scenes worldwide today as people have been converging on abandoned churches. Mass congregations have been spotted holding mobile phones in the air. The reason is unknown, but some accounts point to a meme being spread on social media."

"Well, that was a good day's work. Thanks to Brus!"

"No problem. It is fascinating experiment. Let's see vhere it leads."

"The only thing left to do now is to send the paper I wrote on how to build the portal to all the major research centres around the world. Unless you guys want to take a trip somewhere before all hell breaks loose?"

Then there was a knock on the door. Brus and Chip looked up in some alarm, but Henryk knew who it was.

"It's just Cass," and went to open the door for his friend who sauntered into the room with his hands in his pockets.

"Hey Cass,' said Fret, "All good?"

"Yeah, but me Mum's actin' odd. She's standing in the garden holding her phone in the air. Dad's worried too, but not that much - he's watching the game."

There was one of those moments when everyone looks at everyone else unsure what to say, but before anything could be said, Henryk came back with his coat on and the two of them ran off into the twilight to play in the nearby field.

"Our meme is afoot! Let's see Chip's beach," said Brus.

Chip grimaced.

"Nice place, but I wasn't in the mood to appreciate it."

"How about we go now? The beach'll be empty because it'll be early morning over there."

"I'll go and set it up," said Chip "How's about I maroon you lot there and spend some time alone with your stock of German beer?"

Brus looked with some concern at the American. With the long history between the two nations, and the recent build-up of tensions, the two were getting along, but were wary.

"It would be vise if we took the portable portal with us now wherever we go."

"Agreed," said Mum.

Chip grinned in his eager and appealing American way and went down into the cellar to set up the main portal, while the rest of them sipped their beer. Five minutes later Henryk and Cass burst in through the door.

“Dad!” said Henryk, “There’s a lot of men down the street in black suits!”

“Policemen?”

“No! They’ve got suits of black armour and guns!”

Everyone looked at each other for a few seconds, and then they all dashed for the cellar, leaving half empty mugs of beer.

“Dad! What’s going on!” said Henryk, scared now.

“It’s alright, we’re just going to the beach! Say goodbye to Cass for now. Thanks Cass, for the warning. Good man!”

“Bye Cass.”

“Cool,” said Cass. Then in an undertone, “Your family is as mad as mine today!” Cass ran off to his own house down the street.

Chip was partway through the preparations downstairs when they all burst in on him.

“Have you connected yet?” said Fret in agitation.

“No. I thought I’d do it properly this time, so I wiped the memory and I’m using an algorithm to…”

“You’re joking! There’s a bunch of marines outside. We’ve got to get out of here in two minutes or we’re finished!’

“Well, for cryin’ out loud! I’ve just wiped the memory! It’ll take 10 minutes!”

“We don’t have 10 minutes. Don’t we have a backup on a memory stick?”

There was a bang from upstairs as the front door was crashed in. Mum held her hair with her hands.

“That’s my house they’re demolishing!”

“Our house!” said Fret, from force of habit, and then he and Brus had to restrain her, otherwise she’d have rushed upstairs to tell the marines off.

“Mum! You always know where everything is: where’s the memory stick with the locations on it?”

“Let go of me. On the third shelf up by the washing machine.”

“Brilliant! What are we going to do now?”

Brus closed and locked the cellar door as they all heard heavy footprints above.

“Hurry up!”

The portal sprang into life as Chip and Fret frantically wrestled with the controls and images of various exotic places appeared in the portal.

“We’ll have to scramble the memory, so they don’t know where we’ve gone.”

“I can do zat,” said Brus, “I have suicide program that counts down and wipes the memory. Very useful in my work.”

“Does it erase it all?”

“Da. We Russians know about scorched Earth method.”

Fret quickly went around collecting papers and stuffing them into his rucksack, while Chip and Brus worked with the computer.

Suddenly, a tranquil beach appeared in the portal.

“Vomen and children first. The Russian way, not nihilistic Western way,” said Brus with a wink at Chip.

Mum was fretting about the noises upstairs, but luckily Henryk stepped through the portal, so with a few curses in Korean that no-one understood she walked through.

“Ah! The basis of our happy marriage,” said Fret.

Chip looked puzzled.

“What is?”

“She always curses at me in Korean, and I don’t understand it.”

Footsteps were now tramping down the stairs to the cellar and Brus got out a gun. Fret looked at him with shock.

“You have a gun?”

“Vhy not?”

Bang! Instead of the basement door, there stood what looked like a US marine. Luckily, and unusually, it was a rather uncertain marine, and he stopped dead. Brus pointed a gun at him.

“Stay there!”

Fret dashed through the portal with a large rucksack. Then Chip stepped through into brilliant sunshine and warm scented air. There was the muffled sound of a struggle back in the cellar and just before the portal closed Brus and the marine jumped through tangled together. When the angle was right, Mum hit the marine very hard on the head with a sandy log and he fell onto the sand.

“How dare you enter my house without permission,” she said.

“Our house,” said Fret exasperated.

The portal closed, but the marine, though dazed, was not yet unconscious.

Chapter 22

On a lonely tree-clad island in the middle of the Pacific, a shortwave radio hissed to itself amid the sea gulls and rolling surf.

"..there have been instances of the hysteria worldwide. The Atlantian, EuroFed, Chinese & Russian presidents have called for calm, but social media has enabled widely separated groups to co-ordinate and so far, the governments of a few nations such as South Korea, Norway and Uruguay have fallen to a group of people who call themselves the Executors of Root Command..."

On the beach were a mismatched set of people. A family of three, a NASA programmer, a Russian hacker and a US marine, who was tied to a palm tree at the edge of the beach.

"What did we do?" said Chip, unnerved by the news on the radio.

Brus shook his head, said,

"Fret here is Martin Luther, that's all."

"Great. We've started another 30 Years War!"

Mum, ever practical, wanted to know what they were going to do with the Marine she'd hit on the head and tied to a tree.

"We'll just leave him here, like we did Chip," said Fret, with a quick grin, pacing up and down.

“One thing bothers me,” said Fret, “There’s the portal and some of my papers in the house. If the US government works out how to operate and make a portal, then I’ll have helped them and not everyone. I want to send my paper all around the world so everyone can do it.”

“Just use the portable portal”, said Chip, “Step across to a cyber caf, login and send your pdf to a few experts.”

“Difficult to do,” said Brus, “Your account may be blocked already. As soon as you login, the NSA vill track you down.”

“Don’t you know someone we can visit who can just send the file?”

“Ethical dilemma: they’ll be hounded by the NSA for sure.”

“Let’s just beam into someone’s office, hijack their computer and send it from there.”

“I won’t be able to send it to many people. I want to send this to everyone, or as many people as possible.”

Brus gave a chuckle.

“If you get me to terminal, I can send it to my friends in Kenig, they’ll send it along to others around globe. Vill spread like vildfire.”

“I like it,” said Fret, “Now we just need a terminal. Somewhere we can go and not get burned.”

It was somewhat unfortunate that the word 'Burn' floated around in the air long enough for Fret to make a sentimental connection to somewhere he had been several times, before travel had become difficult. When on the run, predictability is unwise.

It was also unfortunate that no-one was paying attention to the marine. Civilians do not fully appreciate the number of exotic places you can hide a transmitter.

Chapter 23

A day passed, and the portable portal was set up under a swaying canopy of palm trees by the beach, tuned to a location just outside the International Space Science Institute in Bern, Switzerland. It had been chosen because Switzerland was one of the most connected countries in the world, and the Institute (or ISSI) was fondly remembered by Fret as being one of the few that had shown interest in his work before his exile.

Brus and Fret were going, the rest would stay, monitoring events through the portal. They stood before the portal as Chip operated it, in anticipation of the cold of the Swiss mountains.

“I’ve been to Berne twice,” said Fret. “Beautiful scenery, and the people are as nice and honest as can be, but it rains a lot.”

“Rain, I can cope with,” said Brus, “but this sunshine is far too intense.”

The portal was switched on, and immediately Swiss rain started falling out of the oval of the portal onto the sand. The sand was so warm that it hissed and spat a cloud of steam up into the air, making the portal look like the entrance to hell, or perhaps, less poetically, a sauna.

Brus was ready to go, but Fret was pacing by the sea.

“You nervous?” said Mum.

"Yes."

"Can you see another way?"

"No."

"You'll be fine, the momentum is with us!"

"That's my wife: always positive."

They stepped through the portal into Berne, on Hallerstrasse just next to the institute. To the left, the majestic Alps rose white-capped into the sky.

"Let's go inside. And no shooting! I like these people."

"Who said anything about shooting?" said Brus.

They entered through the swinging doors, where a couple of bored policemen were sitting and talking in gutteral Swiss German. They were fairly old policemen and by the time they'd stood up, Brus had drawn his gun.

"Am Platz. Jetzt!" he shouted, and when they hesitated he shot one of the nice white tiles on the ground to emphasize the point. Unfortunately, the bullet bounced off the tile and hit the lower leg of one of the policemen. The poor man screamed and collapsed on the ground and the other one's eyes bulged wide with fear. He raised his hands as if he was trying to escape through the roof.

"What are you doing?!" said Fret to Brus, going to help the policeman.

“Sorry,” said Brus, “but I do not like policemen anyway!”

“What did he ever do to you?”

“Vell, he would have arrested me. Fret, we are not going to get far if you act like Mother Teresa.”

“Likewise with you behaving like Wyatt Earp.”

“Vhat about these two policemen? They’re going to radio in as soon as we leave. Take their radios.”

That done, Fret and Brus dashed up the stairs, and through a door onto the first-floor coffee area. There was a pristine library to the left, a coffee making machine to the right and a terminal on the far wall. A scientist was sat at it, typing slowly on the keyboard, but not for long.

“Ah, come to Mummy!” said Brus to the terminal. He yanked the scientist out of the way as if he was merely a pot plant.

“Was ist Ihr problem!” said the scientist from the floor, with, Fret thought, some justification, but Brus was not to be distracted.

“Wir sind terroristen!” he shouted, pointing his gun at the poor man who squeaked and crawled backwards into an office. Brus immediately clicked on the browser and logged into his email service, while plugging in the memory stick. It was done in less than two minutes. Fret’s paper detailing exactly how to reproduce the portal was sent to fifty of Brus’ online friends with express instructions to send it on to their friends.

"It's done," he said, and both he and Fret burst into excited laughter, which didn't last long as at that moment several more serious policemen burst through the door and took up strategic positions at various points.

"Stand away from that terminal!"

"Blyad!" said Brus, and slowly stood up and moved away.

Immediately the clatter of machine gun fire echoed round the small, sterile room as the police blasted the computer into pieces. Bits of plastic ricocheted around the room and smoke drifted along the floor.

"Too late. We sent it already."

"No, we control the server. Your email's gone nowhere."

The scientist peered wide eyed out of his office, opened his mouth to say something, but saw the troops, thought better of it, and disappeared.

A tall pair of shoulders with a body attached, motioned for the troopers to put their guns down and walked forward towards Fret and Brus.

"Which one of you is Fret?" he asked.

"Who's asking?" said Fret, still gazing in amazement at the smouldering remains of the computer.

"You have some explaining to do, Doctor."

"Do I?"

"Yes. Take a look at this."

He held up a photograph of Fret basement, where the experiment had been. It was still intact as far as Fret could see. Henryk's Lego was still on the floor where it had been and the portal was still standing there like a golden arch, but around the arch there was something new, a shimmering effect, almost as if the light from behind was being refracted in a very uneven manner. Fret pointed to it.

"What's that arc of light there?"

"Indeed. That is the problem."

"What's wrong with my portal? It never showed such an effect when it was switched on before."

"It's not switched on."

"What?"

"We've had soldiers in your basement ever since we got there. There are strange effects, dark ghosts, rings of light and we've had to take some of the soldiers away for psychological testing. We don't understand it, but there appears to be a crack in space-time around your machine, and dark shapes are moving in it. Hence, we've been looking for you, but you have been annoyingly absent. Do you know what is causing this?"

"No. I never expected this. Sure, I'm temporarily deleting space, but I guess I just assumed that when I connected the two parts together again, they would fit.

What I guess might be happening is they don't fit together again at a bit level."

"So can you fix it?"

Fret appeared to be busy with some internal calculations. Shoulders simply stared at him patiently for a while.

"Oh bugger," said Fret.

"Problem?" said Shoulders.

"How about Mars?" said Fret.

"Yes, Mars too. Your apple?"

"Maybe."

"It might be a good time to start being frank with me. I would personally like to rip you into shreds for the crime of potentially destroying the Solar system. Instead, I have to take you to CERN, which isn't far from here, where you can work out a way to fix this. There's a whole group of fascinated scientists waiting there for you."

Brus was staring at Fret.

"We fix the vhorld order and you destroy the Solar system?"

"Well, it's not all bad," said Fret uncertainly, "at least CERN are finally paying attention to my work!"

Chapter 24

The journey to the CERN particle accelerator would have been breath-taking if the occupants of the troop transport had been in the mood, or if they had been able to see it clearly. As it was, it was only visible out of the back of the military APC (Armoured Personal Carrier) and the topography was mostly sensed via the centrifugal force as they rounded numerous bends in the road, a few green faces, and a slow increase of pressure on the ears as they descended. Fret sat with a pad of paper, making sketches and calculations and mumbling to himself incoherently. Brus kept quiet, feeling sick, and missing the delightful flatness of the north European plain. The troops all around them chatted and bantered like troops anywhere in the world. As Brus stared out of the back of the truck at the beautiful alpine scenery he found it hard to imagine that all of that might soon disappear into a crack in space-time. Alpine cottages, gone. Mountain goats, gone. Sky: gone.

When they arrived at the glass-fronted entrance to CERN, there was a crowd of scientists standing outside the place. Not cheering and not jeering, just wanting to catch a glimpse of the physicist who had been ridiculed ten years before and had then gone on to potentially destroy the Solar system accidentally.

Fret kept his face neutral as he walked through the mostly silent crowd with his bodyguard and into the entrance hall of CERN which was a little anti-climactic: grey and square. There were then a few jeers from the crowd outside. An older man came up to him and said,

“Well, Fret. You finally got somewhere.”

Fret seemed to awake from a reverie.

“Professor Unz! It’s good to see a friendly face. Are they finally going to employ me then?”

“I wouldn’t bet on it.”

Another small group of scientists then arrived and introduced themselves as Fret’s tiger team. The head of CERN came over and introduced them, beaming proudly.

“We have a lovely diverse team for you.”

Fret screamed internally at this.

“Yes, but are they good?” said Fret, unwokedly.

There was an uncomfortable pause and a stiffening of attitude, but Fret suspected that he was now in the driving seat and could say whatever he wanted. The leader of the Tiger Team came forward.

“We already have a theory. It’s based on general relativity, and we think this effect is caused by fuzzy dark matter...”

Fret laughed, but not cruelly, more in the manner of someone who has had enough of lazy logic.

“Alright, look, there is no dark matter, all you need is to consider the Cinderella of physics: information, and if you want proof of that statement you can go and look at my basement!”

The group stood with their mouths open until Fret simply had to giggle, then immediately felt guilty and held his hands up in a peace gesture. The Tiger Leader grit her teeth,

“Well, OK. How do you explain the glitches around the portal?”

“I’m not going to say anything, until I’ve seen the data. I appreciate your help and I’d like you to collate some data for me. I need to know when the effect started, its dimensions, whether it affects local gravity, what happens when you fire a laser through it, how fast time passes close up to it and most important whether it is emitting radiation. Can you get that data for me?”

“If you’re so clear about the data you need, can’t you tell us what your theory is?”

“No. Data first, theory second. That was good enough for pre-1933 physics and it’s worked well so far for me, well, except for possibly destroying the world.”

There was nervous laughter and they indicated he should follow them.

“We’ll take you to the place you’ll be working. We have a fat data link to your basement, and we can take the measurements you need.”

“I’d like my family brought here.”

“It would help if we knew where they are.”

"They're on a little island in the Pacific. I just need to phone them and they'll get here."

The open plan office that had been set up for the so-called Gateway project had had much thought put into it. There were the usual desks and terminals, but also bean bags and rich carpets and along the walls were video links showing what the basement phenomenon looked like in real time. Fret's desk was in a cubical that made it a private area, and covered with plots showing various data, including a few of the things he'd asked for.

Left for a while to his own devices, loneliness and fear descended heavily. Fret had experienced it before, when thrown out of academia years earlier partly for having strange ideas. Then he'd felt it, but with the development of his family he had forgotten it. The ending of foreign travel, and wars in Eastern Europe had isolated everyone even further. Now, his family were far off on a Pacific island, and he was responsible for by far the worst potential catastrophe in human history. This was not a thing that he could face on any level directly, so he decided to think about the data instead. As usual the hopefulness generated by working on the problem ended the loneliness and fear.

The data almost immediately did not make sense. Lasers fired into the chaotic area were deflected completely at random. And that meant...

"I'm going for a walk."

His walk lasted until he found the CERN bar and he bought a single beer to both commiserate and celebrate. He may have had to endanger the Solar system to do it, but at least he was now being taken seriously.

Chapter 25

Professor Unz found Fret in the bar about two hours later and sat down in the very precise way he had about doing everything.

“So Fret. Here we are with a big problem.”

Fret was in a more relaxed mood and was drawing interlocking grids on pieces of paper, surrounded by calculations. The world was looking far better than it had.

“I think everyone is misjudging this. It’s a fantastic opportunity to learn more about the world and gain more control over it.”

“How many beers have you had?”

“Too few! I suppose you want to know what causes the phenomenon?”

“Not just me.”

“OK. When I deleted space with the portal, all was fine. This deletes information, pushing entropy down, so, to keep the Gods of physics happy, heat must be released to push entropy up again, but that just goes to warm the room. The problem is when the space reappears from our point of view. This produces new information, does not release heat but the new grid may not align with the existing one.”

“You corrupted space-time?”

"More like the matrix... I think it's worse than that. Imagine you have the binary sequence (he wrote it down) '11110110' which encodes a certain physical state, like spatial DNA. Now the portal effectively sets the right hand side to zero, so it becomes 11110000. Now the passage of time adds a pattern to the left hand side so you get 01010000, Now when you add the original right hand side back in you get 01010110'. The right hand side has missed the update. I have confused it, and it might well be coding something it is not supposed to, something unnatural."

"That would explain the change in the speed of light."

"It might explain the shapes they are seeing in it as well."

"Beings from another dimension?"

"As you know I'm not fond of other dimensions. Not a testable idea, something more in line with glitches in the matrix, but I'm open to all possibilities at the moment. Who knows what combinations of 0s and 1s code for?"

"If it is a higher dimension, is it a danger?"

"No. Different physics. Would you know how to embed into a plane?"

"How many places have you ported to?"

"Tenerife, London, a Pacific Island and we visited Mars, which is how NASA and the Americans found us of course."

"Ah yes. The apple on Mars. Cute idea."

"You know about that?"

"It's been rumoured, but I didn't know you rescued Jon Luther. It's limited to the Solar system then?"

"Not quite. You won't believe it, but we visited another planet, orbiting Tau Ceti, met some aliens…"

Unz spluttered into his beer.

"Now you're pulling on my leg."

"I said you wouldn't believe it. I've spent my life telling people what is perfectly and simple-mindedly true and having no-one believe it."

"Well, with you the truth is always so extraordinary!"

"I suppose. By the way – where is Alex Otz?"

"He was fired for inappropriate behaviour."

"Damn. I was hoping to have a chat with him about Landauer's principle. How about Zbigniew Drapp?"

"Fired for offensive comments. You'll find those left to be a pretty dull lot."

"Yeah, diverse in identity but in lock step intellectually."

"It's been like that for many years."

At that moment, far in the distance could be heard chanting, and as they listened, over a few minutes it got closer and more distinct.

"Don't tell me – a dark matter cult?"

"A cult, yes, but you might like this one. They call themselves Executors of Root Command, or Rooters. Don't know how that got started but it seems to be growing, even at CERN, but only among the non-scientists so far. Now Rooters are not dull..."

The chanting could be heard more clearly now and was rhythmic. The participants were having a lot of fun with it, and phrases such as 'Root command!', 'We're not equal!' and 'Good acts unlock higher levels,' could be heard.

They watched the group pass by. The participants were all holding their phones in the air. Fret knew better than anyone else what was going on and proceeded to explain the alien meme to Unz, once he had bought him a few beers to open him up, just a little bit.

"Well, I never. In fact, it's a bit like your theory isn't it? Un-actioned virtue does not exist?"

The evening wore on in the CERN Bar. The bartender, one of the best educated of his profession, was very careful to mind his own business, but nevertheless couldn't help but hear raucous laughter coming from the two scientists sitting at a table in the corner. CERN is not much of a place for drunken laughter, so it was memorable.

He was also in a good mood. A few hours earlier some men had come to see him and asked whether they could install microphones under all the tables, something that was illegal, but the barman had just gone through a court case in which his wife had taken most of his money so he was finished with the 'system' and was willing to let something like that pass for a tidy few thousand Euros.

He didn't believe all the mantras the Rooters were spouting about good deeds and winning. It sounded like Christianity for gamers. If life were a game, he'd decided, it was more like Poker.

Chapter 26

The next morning, with a hangover, Fret was woken as usual by Henryk jumping on him.

“Dad! We’re back from the island!”

“Hurray! It’s good to see you!”

“D’you know? I found lots of beetles there, and Mum let me bring them along.”

A shiver went down Fret’s spine.

“You didn’t bring them into my bed did you? Like you did last summer?”

“No, silly Dad! I’m much older now.”

Mum was there also, standing by the bed, looking like thunder.

“What’s this about you destroying the world?”

“Oh, that. It‘s overblown.”

“How’s Henryk going to go to university if the planet has disintegrated?”

“Look, dear. I’m starting to lose my positive mood here!”

Luckily at that moment, Unz came in and, winking at him, politely managed to escort Fret’s bristling wife out of the room, leaving Fret and Henryk grinning at each other.

"Dad. It's so cool you worked out how to demolish the Solar system, but do you think you can stop it now? I don't mind but Mum's pretty upset, and my ears are tired."

"Yes, but I don't know how yet. Did you enjoy the island?"

"Well, I did miss my Lego."

After Fret had dressed and returned to his office, with Henryk burbling happily alongside him, he decided he had the guts to check his emails. The number 1836 appeared, and he decided he had more important things to do.

Instead, he decided to set up a conference as soon as possible, to explain to everyone what he had done and what might be possible as a solution. So, he asked how to send a group email to everyone at CERN and sent the following message:

Subject: Introduction to the new physics

Dear All,

I'd like to invite you all to a conference today in the main lecture room at 11am, at which I will explain the new physics and we can then discuss options.

Fret

The sense of power this gave him was immense. The time-tablers of CERN immediately emailed him to say they'd booked the main lecture theatre for a whole day and put on a buffet as well. Steven Hawkyng and Leonard Susskind would fly in to attend. He sat back and looked at Henryk who was building a Lego portal.

“All these years I’ve been nice to people and they ignored me. It seems all you have to do is cause disaster and everyone becomes co-operative!”

“Dad. I’m six, and I’ve known that for ages!”

Chapter 27

The huge auditorium was full of CERN scientists, men in white shirts, women in colourful clothes. Hair colours were of all shades: black, brown, blonde, red and white. All chatting amongst themselves making snide comments about the likelihood of anything useful coming from a conference. A few locked in debate about Root Command. Others were saying that this scare was probably just another excuse to get some funding and that this Brit was probably in it for the money, and isn't that him standing on the stage with his son?

It was him. Fret was stood on the stage with Henryk. Both looking out at the assembled crowd, Henryk in awe, Fret with mixed feelings. It had been at just such a conference, 12 years ago, when he had presented a theory, a new cosmological model for inertia that eliminated the need for the arbitrary and unfalsifiable big bang and dark matter[6], and almost immediately uproar had gone up in the hall. Fret had stood there in shock as normally quiet scientists, and admittedly normally loud cosmologists, had stood up together to hurl abuse his way.

The chair of the session had worked then for five minutes to calm everyone down and asked Fret to make a final statement. This had been his chance to

---

[6] In our universe a similar theory can be seen in papers on quantised inertia: McCulloch, M.E., 2017. Galaxy rotations from quantised inertia and visible matter only. ApSS, 362, 149.

say something witty to win them over but the only thing he had been able to think of was 'Dark matter is rubbish!'

Immediate uproar again, and this time Fret had simply run from the stage. Luckily, the conference was being held in Nice, France and there were some good hills nearby that provided an escape from everyone else. He had ended up in the hill-top village of Eze marvelling at the view, but bad news travels fast and this along with his tendency to speak the simple truth got him fired, giving him lots of time to pursue his work and, as it turned out, endanger the planet.

'They should have listened to me earlier,' he said to himself. 'Yes, and then I'd have destroyed the planet sooner and we wouldn't have needed to be here.', but then he looked at his son and changed his mind. His wife was right: he had to save the planet if Henryk was going to live on it.

The chair of the conference was white haired, and slim. She was the president of CERN, thought Fret, but he wasn't impressed with that sort of thing. Sensing this, she ignored him and went immediately to Henryk.

"Well, young man. Are you enjoying being at CERN?"

"Not really. There's no Lego here."

"Oh yes there is," she said, "Hasn't your father taken you to the children's room?"

"No," said Henryk, looking at Fret accusingly.

"Sorry. I didn't know there was one!"

The head of CERN looked at Fret suspiciously.

"I hear you found the bar easily enough! You should take him. I set the thing up. We have Lego, and snakes and ladders and one of those Z-Boxes…"

"Hey, Dad. I wanted one for Christmas. Can we go?"

"Sure, but not right now."

Then she turned to Fret, polite, but her jaw line was rigid.

"Shall we start? I hope your slides are all ready."

Fret gave a half hour presentation, describing in theoretical terms, but not technical detail, how to set up an event horizon in the basement. How that had deleted a slice of space behind the it, enabling them to travel to, or view, Tenerife, Mars and Tau Ceti (he didn't mention Luther), and ended pointedly by saying how this all grew out of a theory that he'd suggested 12 years ago. He finished to absolute silence and a few stilted coughs.

One hand went up from someone standing next to a wheelchair.

"Professor Hawkyng would like to make a brief statement," said Hawking's assistant, and indeed, there was Professor Hawkyng, in the front row. Immediately the person holding the microphone dashed across the hall to Hawkyng and held the microphone to his computer speaker. The famous rasping voice sounded out across the hall.

"It seems that you have brought information into physics in a rather dramatic way, but unfortunately it is difficult to decide whether you deserve a Nobel prize, or a prison sentence. Do you have any solutions yet?"

"No, I have no solution as yet, but I am convinced there is one."

"Have you considered what this new data means for the black hole information paradox?"

"Yes. It means that the information stored in objects falling into black holes can be destroyed, which is not what standard physics says."

A slow smile spread across Hawkyng's face.

"That was also my guess. I thought I had lost my bet to John Preskill, Susskind and t'Hooft. I hope the world lasts long enough for them to agree that I won."

A gentle American accent sounded from the back of the hall.

"Don't get your hopes up!"

There were many more questions, after Hawkyng had finished, but the physics was too new to the mainstream physicists (though, oddly, it would not have seemed that odd to Ernst Mach, the early Einstein, or Heisenberg) so that the questions were mostly on points of understanding, gratifying in itself, but no advances were made. By the end of the day Fret was exhausted, especially after having had a ritual pre-bed mock-fight with Henryk. Fret went back to the bar, going slowly through his emails fuelled by beer.

One email in particular caught his attention. He immediately erased it, but eventually came back to it because of that old friend - curiosity.

Dear Professor,

Your problem may have happened before, a long time before. Not easy to believe I know but the information may be of help to you. I am in Geneva. If you wish to meet, please reply.

A well-wisher.

Chapter 28

The Jardin d'Anglais was a green oasis in a white city and looked out on Lake Geneva with its famous fountain. Persuading the authorities to allow him to come here had been difficult since they were convinced that the sender of the email, who was apparently from Peru and lived in Dresden, was a crank. He was a museum curator with some odd friends (thank you NSA) and was not to be trusted, but something about Fret's past made him susceptible to this sort of thing.

A scientist appears to be logical, but this is only the front they put on to persuade others. What actually goes on in the head is anything but logical, and ever since Fret had discovered much, he'd begun to notice that a lot of it sounded like ancient legends. Of course, there is the danger of seeing patterns in old scripts that mean nothing. Humans, and even Isaac Newton, who spent the latter part of his life analysing the Bible, are very prone to pattern-forming. Fret was similarly flawed in this way, but realised also that often the right ideas come from the wrong beginnings. So, he persuaded them to let him go to the garden, with a suitable escort of police marksmen who would accompany him from a distance.

He found the clock, made, of course, out of flowers on a grassy bank, under a sky so blue. There indeed was a quintessential Peruvian, with a poncho and large Sun hat. He was stood looking at the clock. He seemed harmless enough. Fret tapped him on the shoulder and he turned revealing a wide Amerindian face and a wide smile.

“Ah. You came! I didn’t think you would!”

“I was intrigued.”

“And desperate?” the Peruvian said with some humour.

“...a little, yes! So, what do you have?”

“Do you know what a codex is?”

Fret’s heart sank.

“It’s a picture book written by the Maya.”

“I can see you are disappointed, and I am sorry for that, but I look after the Dresden codex, one of only three Maya books left in the world. It’s in Dresden of course. I know it by heart and when I saw a news report about you and your machine, I noticed a connection.”

He held up an A4 sheet of paper on which was photocopied what looked passably like the round structure of the portal in Fret’s basement, with cracks emanating from it and in the far right something that looked like a skull was apparently vomiting on the whole thing.

“What is this skull doing?”

“That is Huracan, the Mayan wind god, who is supposed to be putting out a fire in space itself.”

“What does that mean?”

"The skull is a symbol from our mythology meaning time."

Fret slowly counted to ten in his head.

"Do you know the problem with ambiguous books like this? It's possible to see whatever you want in them. I'm sorry, although I've enjoyed some of von Däniken and Graham Hancock, I think you're wasting my time."

The Peruvian did not seem too disheartened by this.

"Please, do allow yourself to be open to possibilities, no matter where they come from, for all our sakes. I think the ancients knew of this and said time will fix it."

"But it could mean a million things."

The part of the Jardin d'Anglais they were in was getting crowded and they both noticed that all the people were looking in the same direction, and muttering. Fret turned to look out upon the lake, the direction of the stares, and thought for a minute he was looking at the fountain.

"That's a pretty tall fountain," he muttered to himself, and indeed it did seem to extend all the way up into space.

"The fountain has been turned off today," said Mr Codex.

"What's that then?"

It wasn't immediately clear what it was, but Fret was sure it was his fault.

The blue sky was being bifurcated by an almost-vertical line, with all the colours of the rainbow in it, and moving slowly along it were pulses of intense light, making it look just like a space elevator for angels.

Fret's phone started playing a pale imitation of Dire Straits' Telegraph road.

"Yes, hello?"

"Fret?" It was Professor Unz, "I think you had better return to base."

"Is this something to do with a crack in the sky?"

"Yes. Something's happened at your home."

"Is it alright?"

"We don't know yet, this happened only five minutes ago. We haven't contacted our group there."

"Where does the line end?"

"Mars! That's one of the places you went isn't it? I'd watch out if I were you. A lot of people are getting mad at you."

Fret closed his phone and turned to talk to the Peruvian, but he had helpfully disappeared.

Chapter 29

The park was emptying now, as people in their confusion and worry made their way home watching The Crack in the sky out of the corner of their eyes. Only a homeless man sat dejectedly by himself by the pathway, next to a tent filled with meticulously-stacked books. Solid and unmoved by the movement around him. As Fret passed by, he said,

“Changer, s’il vous plaît?”

“I only have a ten Euro note.”

The homeless man, of course, knew English.

“No problem. I can give change.”

Fret stopped in mid heart beat.

“Say that again?” he said.

“I say ‘Do you have change?’ I’ll pay it back.”

Fret simply stood there in sudden internal shock. The homeless man was extremely pleased at the number of coins that Fret gave him, saying,

“Thank you! You’ve saved my life.”

“Hey, that’s my line is it not?” said the homeless man.

“Not today! Today you saved my bacon.”

The homeless man took this in and showed a shrewd understanding of business that make Fret wonder what the hell he was doing homeless.

"If I've saved your life, then maybe it's worth even more than this?"

"Yes, alright."

Fret opened his wallet again.

"Here's a couple of 50 euro notes. All I have. Use them wisely."

"Merci! By the way, what did I do?"

"You reminded me of Heisenberg: that line up there in the sky is now there because I borrowed some lack of space from the future."

The homeless took this confusing statement surprisingly well.

"Bah! Heisenberg! Matrix mechanics! I can predict the allotropic forms of hydrogen without those clumsy tools."

"You know some physics do you?"

"I wasn't always on the street. I used to work at CERN. Then I was fired by those woke people."

Fret stared at his eyes, the only part of him not covered by a white beard.

"Professor Otz?!"

"I used to be."

Fret gave him his watch as well.

"Listen, it's a long story but the woke craze has been replaced by a healthier one. I saw to that. Get back to CERN! Now I need to talk to you about something..."

Professor Otz indicated down the street with his head.

"I prefer living on the street, so interesting! I'll be here, if here continues to exist, but it looks as if someone's taking an interest in you."

Fret turned to see several Swiss policemen, with blue-black uniforms and truncheons, walking rapidly towards him, looking sideways rather nervously, it must be said, and with firearms. Their leader stood in front, with the others behind, hands on pistols as if Fret was just about to release a barrage from a machine gun concealed in his hat.

"Doctor Bohrson?"

"Yeerrss?"

"I'm Officer René Calvin. We have orders to arrest you for the crime of...," the policeman checked with his clipboard "...comprehensive genocide."

Professor Otz gave a slow whistle.

"Wow! That's some crime. I only touched a woman's knee. Are they serious or is this a joke by your wife?"

"They're serious, but wrong. I've just realised that the human race will be fine ...but I might not."

Professor Otz looked pleased at this.

"Sehr Gut. I'll have time to spend this then!"

The policemen had now managed to arrange themselves into a semi-circle that precluded Fret's escape.

"Sir," said the policeman, "These charges are real but I also need to take you in for your own safety. The Executors of Root Command want to talk to you, most people want to lynch you, and God knows what some of the other weirdos want."

Chapter 30

Swiss prisons were as clean as their reputation, but not particularly interesting. Nevertheless, the boredom they were filled with was an advantage in one sense. Surrounded by people at CERN Fret had had very little time to think, but after 48 hours in solitary confinement in the prison he worked a lot out on the tiny pad he always carried. The path forward was simple but, as so often in life, before he'd had a chance to appreciate that, another, more immediate problem appeared.

The chanting started shortly after he'd been incarcerated. At first it was impossible to understand what it meant, His guard was a friendly Swiss-German who translated it as something like

"Death to the cosmos killer."

"What does that mean?"

The guard looked uncomfortable.

"Oh, zey accuse you of destroying the cosmos. Zey think it is all cracking apart and you are to blame."

"Are they serious?"

"Vell, you must admit, zey look up at the sky, see this crack from the Earth to Mars and zey vonder."

"Wonder what?"

"If it's going to crack further."

"I see."

"Is it going to crack further?"

"No!"

"Vell, zat's alright then, but if I were you, I'd broadcast that information a little more widely. They say they're going to lynch you, so we've drafted in more guards from Basle and Bern to protect you."

"We're safe in here then?"

"No. Swiss people have guns. Zey could easily break in."

After this conversation Fret had been unable to sleep. The crowd outside was also apparently unable to sleep and they kept up their chanting and occasional rocks hit the barred window of Fret's prison cell.

Then, in the middle of the night there was a large explosion and shouting in French and German, and what sounded like Spanish. The guard came running over to Fret's cell in a state of panic.

"Zey're coming!" he hissed.

Shouts echoed in the corridors. There were several sharp bangs as they shot away the lock on the door at the end of the corridor and then the mob streamed in. The guard said a quick,

"Sorry! Bon chance,"

and dashed off down the corridor to save himself.

Chapter 31

The main news today from Radio Atlantia. There have been peaceful marches all over the world. This time they are not the work of the many varieties of the so-called woke movement that has been dominant of late, but from groups who call themselves the Executors of Root Command, or, more recently, the Rooters or Actioneers. In the studio we have Martin Johns, Professor of Social Studies at the University of Wittenberg to explain.

"Professor, can you please characterise this movement for us?"

"Yes Angela. The Actioneers' philosophy, which, by the way spread quickly from an unconfirmed source on social media, is directly opposed to wokism. Actioneers or Rooters believe that people should be judged upon their actions alone."

"Would you say the movement is like a religion?"

"Possibly. It may be the first technological religion, because Actioneers regard the world as something like a computer game, in which good acts are a manifestation that the individual's soul deserves elevation to the next level up."

"What happens when they elevate?"

"The idea is that the world reforms around you in a slightly better version, rather like the idea of heaven, but immediate, and with gamer overtones and infinite levels."

“What has convinced so many people so quickly?”

“A combination of the fast spread of the supposed message of Root Command made possible by social media, & the miracle of these cracks in the sky seems to have accelerated it.”

“How is the world economy reacting to all this?”

“Well, oddly it has been noticed that in most areas productivity and social cohesion are improving as hard work and kindness are good acts and people are performing these good acts more often. Maybe this is a new Protestantism. Who knows?”

“Well, thank you very much Professor. I hope your kind explanations today gain you a step up to the next level!”

“Thank you. Maybe my contribution today will mean I’ll wake up driving a BMW.”

“You never know!”

Chapter 32

It has been shown that the toxoplasmosis parasite in rats, inhibits the fear centre of their brain, the amygdala, freeing them of fear to such an extent that they go looking for cats.

Fret was just considering whether all his career problems could be explained in a similar manner, and whether he should get medically tested, when a group of, very un-Swiss men crowded round his cell. They looked more like South Americans than Europeans. One called out with a Spanish accent,

"Chill Amigo. We are here to help!"

"Help who?" said Fret.

They smiled gleefully at that, but then apologised very profusely and shot him. He looked down at the dart protruding from his leg, and felt dizzy.

"Funny sort of help," he said, and slowly the world started to spin in a way very different to the usual slow eastward rotation. From his point of view the South Americans turned into cats and began a slow dance before smashing up through the ceiling, letting in a bright light that, just as much as perfect darkness, obliterated everything.

Chapter 33

There is a theory that eighty years after a major war, all the people who were trained to high common sense in that period of crisis die off, and those born post-war with less common sense cause a new war, and so the cycle continues. [7] Cycles of death and rebirth also occur within individual human lifetimes and they may also occur on timescales of tens of millennia as well, but there the historical record is unfortunately silent.

Warm face - Intense sunlight in the eyes - tropical bird calls outside. The sunlight on Fret's face woke him up. It was coming from a small window in an ancient large-stoned wall. Its sunbeam had slowly changed its angle till it was shining directly on his face, like an alarm clock operated by the Solar system. Slowly he sat up. No pain. He got up, and the ground wavered in a very un-ground-like manner.

Nevertheless, he was determined to get to that window and find out where he was, because, given the intensity of the sunlight he was unlikely to be in sun-starved northern Europe, and the tropical birds singing outside the window were another interesting clue.

Eventually he got to the window and looked out, but peering into the sunlight all he could make out were distant mountains, not floating this time, and a uniformly blue sky.

---

[7] Strauss & Howe, 1997. The Fourth Turning.

"Where the hell am I?" he asked himself, his voice echoing in the Spartan room.

"You are safe and in Manchu Picchu," boomed a voice from behind him.

He whirled. Standing there in the doorway was the man he had met in the Jardin Anglais.

"You? But that's in Peru!"

'So are you. We kidnapped you – for your own safety."

"Yes, that's what your posse said, just before they shot me."

The man opened his hands wide.

"I'm sorry about that, but you were about to be lynched by an angry Swiss mob, so we had to get you out and make it look like we were going to lynch you first."

"Well…thanks?"

The man stuck out his hand.

"My name is Sergio. Welcome to Peru!"

"Thank you. How do I get back home?"

"Soon. We have something useful to tell you, for which we do have evidence."

"This isn't another codex is it?"

"No. Something a little more ancient."

He held up a small ring, about the size of a doughnut and asked a question.

“What size is your smallest portal?”

“1.2 metres across.”

He then put his hand through the ring and it appeared about a metre from the ring.

“This portal is about 10 cm across.”

“Well, you’ve obviously progressed a lot. We didn’t shrink it further because there’s no point.”

“We didn’t do it,” said Sergio, “This ring was found in what was thought to be a tomb deep beneath Gunang Padang in Indonesia. It is the only one of its kind. When you invented your portals, we experimented on it, powered it up and found that this was a very ancient portal, and not jewelry as had been supposed.”

“What do you mean ancient?”

“About 12 thousand years old according to carbon dating.”

“Come again?”

“I’m going to show you something now that is also very ancient, and very advanced. You only need to put this on your head.”

He held out a silver-white object that looked like a scull-cap.

"It looks very modern."

"Yes, but it is also very ancient. Again, it was found in Gunang Padang. We, er, stole it. Put it on your head."

"Is it safe?"

"You have my guarantee. If we wanted to harm you, we'd have done it already. It's simply a kind of direct-stimulation virtual reality, but very advanced."

Fret put the hat on his head, instantly the room disappeared and was replaced by a landscape that was undoubtedly something like the Andes, but which had what appeared to be mountains, even cities floating in the sky.

"Beautiful! I saw something like that recently…"

"Where?"

"Oh, very far away from here."

"They are floating cities," said the Amerindian, "by carbon dating associated organics we've found it, again, to be about 12,000 years old. You can move around to some extent and see what their world was like. It's a bit like google Earth. You can zoom out to look at the world from space and then zoom in to anywhere. Just imagine doing it, see the rough image in your head, and the device will work out what you're willing it to do."

Fret zoomed out into space and spanned the globe to find Europe. The UK was joined to the continent so that the English Channel was just a large estuary. Scotland was under ice, as was Scandinavia, and the Sahara was not a desert, it was a green savannah, full of cities. The Caribbean, Mediterranean and Indonesia were also different. They had far more land and were also covered with coastal cities, all with some floating buildings. The changes in coastlines were hardly a surprise to him, since he'd known the sea level was lower during the ice age, far more water being locked up in polar ice, but, cities? Fret zoomed in towards the Egyptian pyramids. They were there, rising out of a tropical jungle, but were coated in brilliant white marble.

Fret took the hat off, thinking that of course it could be some elaborate hoax.

"Neat technology, putting images directly into the brain, but how do I know any of these images represent real history and not a hoax? And how has it lasted so long in good condition?"

"It's an advanced alloy. I merely show it to you. You're a scientist, so you should know about the importance of evidence and correct citation."

"Yes, but if there was such an advanced civilisation on Earth, 12,000 years ago, then why have we not seen more evidence of it? DVDs, modern buildings and old settlements on the Moon for example?"

"Imagine our civilisation collapsed. Would our DVDs survive for thousands of years? Modern materials are designed to become obsolete quickly, even these days biodegradable, so if we did vanish from history a future civilisation may well think that we gave up after building the cathedrals in Europe."

"How about the New York skyscrapers?"

"Concrete only lasts for 100 years at most."

"Alright. Good point."

"No matter. We deciphered some old texts. We did not understand them until the recent events, but as I showed you, these ancient engineers also built portals like yours..."

"So, I'm not the first?"

"In such a large cosmos as ours, it's unlikely you'd be first."

Fret said nothing to this, but silently fumed.

"The important message is that these texts imply that the rends in space caused by your use of the portal occurred before, for these people when they invented the portals. And shortly afterwards their civilisation collapsed."

"Great. Now I'm not the first, and still responsible for destroying the cosmos?"

Sergio smiled.

"All things work together for good. We believe that. Also, as a word to the wise, they may have left the Earth thousands of years ago – so watch out for them!"

"I'd have liked being a librarian. Think of all that peace and blessed insignificance."

"I have to warn you of some of the things they mention in these texts. These cracks, they can be dangerous. Not because they linger, they don't."

"That's what I suspect. They heal up..."

"Yes, but before that there can be a lifeform in them. Something from outside our kind of space."

Chapter 34

It is possible that the cosmos started off as a random mess. Over time, any processes that happened to repeat, such as waves, orbits, or life, became locked in, and these are what we now called physics, but what if parts of the cosmos were given a severe shake and latched onto an entirely new set of repeating processes. What then?

Sergeant Lewis was not a happy man. He'd been sitting in the dusty basement for several hours looking at the kaleidoscopic doughnut that now stood where the portal was. It was fascinating in that all sorts of different colours and shapes were forming within it, but at some point it seemed to him that the colours and patterns suddenly became consistent and sparks began to fly. Lewis phoned his supervisor who was in a café in the centre of town, by the river with a rather nice blonde.

"Yes, Bellevue here. What is it? I'm busy."

"Captain, I think you'd better come and have a look at the portal. It's changed."

"In what way has it changed?"

"It's sparking!"

"Sparking?"

"Yessur, and I'm getting nervous."

"Look Sergeant, I'm rather busy at the moment, wink, wink. Maybe the sparking will pass eh?"

"It's been going on for ten minutes now sir."

"Ten minutes? What's ten minutes! Call me in forty-five."

Sergeant Lewis put his phone down and looked nervously at the portal, spoke miserably to himself.

"Bellevue's always the same. Probably off with some blonde while I'm sitting here minding the portal to hell. Story o' my life."

Chapter 35

Chip was getting bored. The atmosphere of impending doom at CERN was so very Olde Worlde, and his optimistic American soul hated it. The imprisonment and subsequent disappearance of Fret was also unnerving, so he was incredulous and extremely pleased to see Fret skyping him, from God knows where. He accepted the call.

"Fret! Where the hell are you?"

"Manchu Picchu, Peru."

"Where? Are you sneezing?"

"No! It's a deserted mountaintop village in Peru. They'll have to send a helicopter."

"We were worried about you – and now you're on holiday!"

"I was kidnapped – look, long story, just send a portal – I have lots to try out."

"We're forbidden to use portals at the moment, so it'll have to be a slow form of transport."

"Can I see my son, is he around?"

"Yeah, he's asleep somewhere round here."

"Can I speak to him?"

After being prodded and woken, Henryk exploded with joy at seeing his dad and told him about the children's room at CERN which was apparently awesome. Meanwhile Chip dashed across the room to organise transport. Manchu Picchu! Even the geography was getting weird.

“Dad, I miss you!”

Thank goodness - some things never change.

Chapter 36

The basement had hardly changed. It was still untidy, and girded with books. The portal had changed. The column of iridescence that was now stretching all the way to Mars had sliced through the ceiling.

“It’s a slice out of spacetime all right,” said Chip.

Waltz Peck, a bureaucrat who had been drafted on them at CERN was in full offensive mode.

“So, Fret. Have you come to a conclusion about this mess that you have plunged the world into?”

Fret sucked his teeth for a second and replied through gritted teeth.

“I know what is happening.”

“I’m listening.”

“You’re not going to believe it, because you’re still in a machine mindset.”

“This isn’t going to be some new age rubbish is it?”

“No, it’s based on data. Look, with the industrial revolution we learned to think about machines and Newton gave us the maths for it. We think in straight lines and assume that the world is running down and energy will all end up as useless heat, just like in a machine.”

“That’s what all physicists think, yes.”

“Not all. I was working on my own for a long time and absorbed a lot of wild ideas, for example from Mach and Einstein of course, but also from Schauberger who believed, like the ancient Greek Thales, that the world and physics was growing and behaved more like biology.”

“On the other hand, when Planck met Schauberger he said that physics had nothing to do with nature.”

“I admire Planck, but he must have been having a bad day. It’s my opinion that the physical laws we have now are just caused by randomness which has by accident found patterns that reproduce, so that the laws we see now are not the only ones possible.”

“Newton’s gravity law is not fundamental?”

“No. In some sense it’s just a pattern that reproduces, like amoebas, frogs, waves, planetary orbits and humans. What repeats, lasts, so now all we see around us are repeating patterns, like DNA. Physics can grow. What I did with slicing up space is to disrupt that pattern or matrix. It has then randomly toppled around and on this occasion has come up with another stable pattern that is different, rather like an environmental catastrophe would cause a rapid change in species.”

“Proof?”

“I can demonstrate that that mess over there is both stable, and obeys different laws of physics to our cosmos, and I did it earlier. See the laser beam passing through it?"

"I see it."

"The usual speed of light is about 300,000,000 metres per second, so fast that it gets to the Moon and back in 2.5 seconds, but the laser beam passing through the anomaly arrives at the detector slightly faster than it should, meaning that while it is in the anomaly it is travelling faster than our speed of light. Actually, if the speed of light is c then the light in the anomaly is travelling at 1.41c."

"Faster than the speed of light?"

"Ours, yes."

"That is impossible!"

"Nothing is impossible that happens. So you see, light speed is a pretty fundamental constant, and here it is different and also stable – I tried it at different locations and times."

"Will this new physics spread?"

"It could overwrite the cosmos like a computer virus."

There was a tension building up in the room at this point.

"Will it then?"

"Maybe."

"Maybe?!"

"I only have a hunch."

"Which is?"

"I'd rather not say, yet, but I think it'll be alright."

"You're very relaxed for a man in your position."

"Funny. My wife is always saying the same thing!"

Chapter 37

The Sun was setting over a beach somewhere in the Caribbean, with style, as only the Caribbean Sun can. The sky was on fire, with so many shades of red and orange that only an insane impressionist, or a well-funded photographer, would be able to reproduce it. The gentle swash of the waves was a pulse that came and went, sometimes faster sometimes slower, but always seeming to be unhurried, and the salty aroma of the ocean wafted inland, cleansing and soothing everything in its path.

There was a family on the beach, the empty beach, looking pretty much like any family might have. Mum was sitting on a carefully sand-less blanket reading a book with a wide brimmed hat on, looking, as usual, like a mushroom. The two boys were building a dam and daring the sea to come and knock it down.

"It's coming Dad," screamed Henryk, as a tiny capillary wave trickled gently towards the dam.

"Don't panic," said Dad, who was attempting to build a channel to draw the water into a pool behind the dam.

The past few days had been blissful, and that was good because Dad had been close to a nervous breakdown, sitting in the basement and staring at a space / matrix that was as knotted as an old oak tree, and being goaded by a crusty CERN handler. He'd decided that after possibly destroying the universe as we knew it, and the social status quo as well, a holiday was in order, and the scientists at CERN, probably keen to get him out of the way, so some 'real' science of the uber-theoretical and untestable form could be applied, had readily agreed to pay for a trip to the Caribbean. Dad had been, from their point of view, infuriatingly calm about the whole thing.

"It'll work out all right," he'd said, to a crowd of raised eyebrows and lynch-like looks. He wasn't sure what gave him the confidence, but it often happened that his unconscious mind appeared to know far more than he did, and he'd learned to trust it. All would be fine, he just had to prove it to everyone else.

It was good to be here, on a private beach, thinking about nothing but dams, because at home there were whole nations of people who'd like nothing better than to string him up. 'That was OK', he thought to himself: pioneers were always misunderstood.

"Dad, it's really coming now. Look!"

Dad looked and was suddenly hit in the face by a large, cold, wet wave.

"What the..."

He looked out to the horizon to see a dark green motor boat moving away fast. The wake from the boat was the cause of the large waves now smashing down their dam.

"Hooligan!"

He looked inland to the east at the 'Crack in the Sky', as it had become known, although it was, of course, a crack in space. He had looked several times but this time he noticed something different. It was definitely brighter.

“It’s just the sky is getting darker,” he said, but a still small voice told him otherwise.

Chapter 38

The Atacama Desert of northern Chile is not a place to get stuck without a water bottle. It is so cloudless and dry that when NASA wants to simulate Martial soil, then that is where they go. It also means that it is a fantastic place to put a telescope without having to worry about clouds.

It was a relaxed day at the Magellan telescopes in Chile, and Enrico Lopez, a budding world-class Argentinian astronomer was having a problem with a colleague of his. Gabriela had always been ascerbic and unpleasant to work with. However, she had just been converted to Rootism, and fanatical with it. Overnight she had gone from feminist icey hostility to a deep warmth and femininity. She was brown-skinned and voluptuous, with dark hair and smouldering looks that were making it difficult for Enrico to concentrate. She virtually bounced into the telescope control room.

“So, have you finished with the big boy today?”

In case you think this is that kind of book, it isn’t! The big boy was the largest telescope at the observatory, a 20 inch Cassegrain: a telescope made of mirrors.

“Yes. You can have control if you like.”

“It’s alright. I’ve other fish to fry.”

“What?”

“Now I have achieved enlightenment, I want to maximise my effect, reach my unique female potential.”

"OK. And what is that?"

"I want to have and raise children, and quick!"

"Why?"

"To get to a higher game level. As Root Command says, I've been on the back foot trying to be a man, when I was born in the game as a woman, and I can beat you all hollow being a woman and get to a more pleasant level!"

"Is this religion based on gaming or something?"

"Sorta," she laughed a throaty laugh he'd never heard, "So, how about it? You have good DNA, a symmetrical face, a PhD. You're kind. Do you want to sleep with me?"

Enrico was a hot blooded and sensible Latin fellow and said "OK," immediately.

"Good. Let's not waste time."

Enrico did his pleasant duty to Gabriela and then at about 2 AM he sneaked out, back to the telescope. The hall echoed coldly as the telescope drivers creaked it into position. The change in the appearance of the crack was striking. It was brighter and there was some detail in it. He was unhindered by the presence of any colleagues, most of whom were away at a conference. It is not every day that you see something so obviously new.

He focused in with the telescope. There were details for sure, most of it was still yellow, but there were now dark shadows, and after a few minutes it was clear that the shadows were moving slowly.

“What the hell are those?”

The observatory phone rang and Enrico picked it up.

“Enrico?” said his boss at the other end of the line, “NASA have just been in touch they want you to turn the Big Boy on The Crack.”

“Already done sir. I’m looking at it now.”

“Can you set up a live feed to them, they want to monitor.”

“Alright, just improving the filter now. What is happening to The Crack sir?”

“I can’t even begin to guess.”

It seemed to Enrico that the shapes moving there had a definite pattern to them, and he began to record them.

Chapter 39

“As many of you may know, since it is visible in the night sky over the western hemisphere, the so-called Crack created by a rogue scientist has today showed disturbing signs of development. We have in the studio today Professor Stephen Hernandez, noted astrophysicist and adviser to the National Institute for Astronomy. Professor Hernandez, is there any theory that says anything about the shapes recently seen in the Crack?”

“Thank you for inviting me for a chat. No, there is no widely-accepted theory that can explain them. The guilty party, I am too enraged to say his name, who has a theory, has not made a statement. I do not believe there is much to go on yet in deciding the cause.”

“But you must, being an expert, you must have some idea what is going on?”

“Well, this is hot off the press, but one thing that has been noticed, by an astronomer in Chile is that the shapes and details, when you take into account the actual distances involved in the Crack which stretches from the Earth to Mars, the shapes in it are moving faster than light, and specifically at 1.41 times the speed of light, in accordance with the different physics that the guilty party predicted and indeed observed recently by passing a laser through the Crack. It is also interesting to me that the shapes appear to drift not along the Crack but across it…”

“What does that mean?”

“It means a great deal. It means that these shapes are possibly not confined to the Crack but represent events occurring in a wider space beyond the crack.”

“Do you mean in another universe?”

“I do. It is my belief, only a belief, that the Crack is indeed a gateway into a higher dimensional universe, or at least another universe that has been opened up, and that we need to close it quickly.”

“Why so?”

“Because something beyond nasty could pay us a visit.”

“OK, well.. er… thank you Professor Hernandez. Let us hope that nothing like that happens!”

Chapter 40

The family had been looking with increasing distress at the Crack. You might think that Fret, being the person who caused the Crack in the first place, would be the best person to work out how fix it, but his mind always had been finely tuned to thinking only about whatever was interesting, and the crisis had shifted the Crack from the interesting category to the horrific category and whenever he tried to think about it, he started to fall asleep. You might say 'Buck up man' but the creative mind is a delicate system and will not operate when forced. Building sandcastles was about Fret's limit at the moment. His phone rang.

"Oh, what now?"

He reluctantly picked it up.

"Fret, It's Unz."

"Hello. The only guy who isn't trying to lynch me."

"You don't know how true that is. I need to warn you, we've just heard here that elements in the US government have decided, completely irrationally that you constitute a terrorist threat and have decided to ...er, take you in. I'm not an expert on these kind of things, but I think you ought to seriously consider, well... hiding."

"But how can they justify that?"

"They are not in a rational frame of mind at the moment, they are just looking for someone to punish, so I'd make myself scarce. They do not know where you are yet. We told them you're on St Kilda... Goodbye and good luck."

The line went dead.

"Oh, blast," said Fret.

"What?" said Mum, looking up from her book.

"I'm in trouble."

Wives have the ability to apply far more guilt than the American army, and she gave him a withering look.

"Why did I marry you? You've been nothing but…"

"Can we have this discussion another time? We need to hide."

"Where are we going to hide? This is a small island!"

Henryk was an expert on this kind of thing.

"Dad! We can hide in the jungle, like Paddington's family. They hid there for years and no-one found them."

Just at that moment there was an ear-splitting noise as a jet flew over the beach.

"Time's up! Quick … into the jungle!"

Mum was indignant.

“Are you crazy? I’m not going in there, I’ve only got my swimming costume on and my shoes are totally wrong...”

“I think you’re going to have to. They’re after me but I’m not sure how selective their aim is going to be.”

“My mother told me you were no good from day one…”

Dad dragged Mum towards the jungle, and Henryk was already in the trees.

“Come on Mum. It’s cool in here!”

It was indeed cool under the trees, and the sound of cicadas heard out on the beach was dulled by the canopy, to be replaced by a whole set of new sounds and smells.

“It sounds like a frog chorus in here,” said Henryk poetically.

Mum was not happy and was looking around her in some alarm.

“Are there any snakes in here?”

“Of course,” said Fret.

Mum stopped and looked at her husband with real loathing.

“Sometimes I just wish you were less honest!”

“Come on, the Americans are coming.”

“Maybe it’s a false alarm?”

There was the sound of a landing craft from the beach at that point. Fret looked at his wife.

“Any questions?”

“Yes. I want a divorce!”

“That’s not a question.”

Chapter 41

Enrico felt like a king, wrapped partially around Gabriella. He had everything he wanted at that moment. She was sleeping and he had a chance to think about what he wanted to do now they were together. Objectively speaking, this new romance was a damn nuisance since he had wanted to go to Europe for a while and bask in the intellectual hothouse of Oxford or Cambridge, but other emotional concerns were now likely to stop that, and what bothered him even more was that he didn't care. He'd rather have Gabriella than anything else. What kind of idiot was he turning into?

Oddly though, he found his mind turning to the Crack. There was something nagging at him, something that had been bugging him all day. Sure, he'd seen patterns, but he hadn't decoded them. Something more to do with the edge of it. It was incandescent with light, more so than the centre which suggested that it was the envelope of the cylindrical Crack that was emitting light. Where was the glow coming from? And all the energy needed to produce it?

"What is it?" he said to himself.

"Hmph," said Gabriella, opening her eyes a crack.

He kissed her full lips, and she smiled and moved against him.

That was enough puzzling for the evening.

Chapter 42

There's a lot to be said for living in a cave. Having solid rock surround you on at least three sides, cuts out the likelihood of attack from those directions, so at least you know where an attack is likely to come from. The problem is there is also only one escape route.

The family had found a cool cave, halfway up the (hopefully) extinct volcano that rose up from the centre of the island and just beyond the tree-line so that from the mouth of the cave there was a glorious view of the northern half, which allowed a view right along its backbone. The land could be seen falling away on either side down to the darker forested areas near the coast and then the abrupt yellow rim of the beaches.

What could also be seen was an American frigate, in the turquoise waters, and the occasional boat could be seen making its way from the ship to the shore.

"What are we going to do Dad?" asked Henryk.

"I don't know, but I want to talk to you, come over here and sit down."

Henryk was by the cave entrance but came and sat down.

"I want you to know that I love you."

"Dad, you're not going away are you?"

"Henryk, please just let me talk."

"Because if you go away that's not like love is it?"

"But it's to save you and Mummy. If I go and give myself up to the marines, then they won't come and harm you."

"Maybe they will. They might get you and then come and get us too!"

"I don't think they would do that."

"What we need is a portal. It was great fun Dad, when we had one. We could go anywhere. Now all we do is just sit in a cave. It's boring here. We don't even have a lightbulb."

"What?"

"I said: we don't even have a lightbulb. It's getting too dark, I can't even draw."

Some instinctive signalling was telling Dad that the insight he'd had earlier by Lake Geneva, was just now colliding with another insight, something to do with a lightbulb. He put his hand to his head in the time honoured fashion of people having a eureka moment and luckily the two ideas collided and he was able to watch it happen.

"Light," he said almost incoherently.

"What is it Dad?"

Dad grabbed Henryk by the shoulders, stared into his face beaming, said,

"Where is the light from the crack coming from?"

“You said it was from another universe.”

“No! The Crack is making it itself!”

“How?”

“Because of Landauer’s principle. And that means there’s a way to reseal it!”

“How Dad?”

“Er... I’m don’t know yet, but at least it is feasible.”

Landauer’s principle was an explosive insight, made by Rolf Landauer, a computer scientist who realised that when you erase computer memory from binary digits of say 1101001 to 0000000 then that is a real reduction of information, entropy or disorder (in this case, electron spins) and, as anyone with a child in the house knows, disorder never decreases – that is a rock solid law of nature. As a result, the erasure of information must always be accompanied by an emission of radiation or heat which is the ultimate in disorder, to keep entropy rising and satisfy the cosmic accountant.

At this point Dad, who hadn’t so much as smiled for days, started dancing round the cave. Mum who had been asleep, woke up, and seeing Dad dancing around said:

“Oh, no. Dad’s had an idea. That means more trouble.”

Chapter 43

Enrico suddenly sat up in bed, elated.

"That's it!" he said as Gabriella mumbled in her sleep.

"Dearest, I feel pregnant."

"That's where the light comes from!"

"What light?"

"The light in the Crack. It comes from Landauer!"

"Where's Landauer?"

"He's a person, or was."

"What are you talking about?"

"No-one's asked the obvious question. No-one ever does! The Crack, where is all the light coming from?"

"Root comm.."

"Oh, bugger root command! Because the Crack is lighter around its edge than in its centre which says to me that it is the edge that is emitting the light, and it's not coming through from the centre."

"But why is the edge emitting light then?"

"Because the Crack is like a sausage in space extending from the Earth to Mars and its surface area is shrinking."

"Hang on. This isn't some sort of erotic afterplay is it?"

“No! This is serious. The sausage is emitting light.”

“Because it is shrinking? Not so romantic...”

“Yes, I read that English guy’s latest paper. He said that the shrinking of a horizon, releases heat energy. That’s what the Crack is doing.”

“So, you mean it’s shrinking?”

“Yes, if only we could boost the light emission!”

“Finally, some good news. Of course, I could have told you that the cosmos will not split up.”

“How so?”

“Root Command would never allow...”

“Oh, you and your Root Command. You’re off your head.”

“Unbeliever,” said Gabriela, but with a warm smile.

“Shame it won’t save that English scientist. He’s been declared persona non grata by the Americans. They’re going to try him for destroying the planet.”

“Well. We’d better let them know they’re over-reacting!”

“Stop Americans? Well, good luck with that!”

Chapter 44

There was a sudden staccato burst of megaphoned American English from outside the cave.

"Doctor Boarson. Please exit the cave. You're under arrest for crimes against humanity."

Fret stopped in mid bounce. The three fugitives looked at each other, faces frozen in indecision.

"Look, I'm going to have to give myself up. The Americans might then pick you up as well, but they're decent generally with people they don't hate, and the guys'll portal to you in time – never mind the ban. I need to convince the Americans that we can fix the problem."

"We'll rescue you, Dad!" said Henryk with feeling.

Fret felt the need to tell his son something momentous. Something along the lines of the Dylan song 'Forever Young', such as "May you build a ladder to the stars, and climb on every rung" or "May you have a strong foundation when the wind of change shift", but trying to think of something good in this mood was never going to work, so he merely tried to tell the truth.

"I love you son, and I'm happy that you will continue, and I really do think you'll be a better man."

Dad brushed Henryk's hair, as if it was the last time he'd be able to do it, as well it might, and turned to his wife.

"Thanks wife. You've been a rock…"

"How romantic. A rock!"

"You've saved my life more than you'll ever know. I love you too…"

She was reassuring, as ever, simply by standing there square and solid. He had always imagined that even a nuclear explosion would fail to budge her. She gave him a playful bump on the arm.

"It'll be alright. I say so, and am I ever wrong?"

"Er... No."

"Well, there you go then. Just promise me you'll survive for long enough that we can get to you. OK?"

Fret took one last look at them and walked out of the cave and into the waiting arms of a lot of beefy, angry and trigger-happy Marines.

Chapter 45

General Naille had been chasing terrorists all his life, and hated them. Why couldn't they fight in the open, on the battlefield like everyone else? But, despite the hatred he had for them, the hatred he had for this fellow was an order of magnitude greater. He hadn't paid much attention in school to the details of the Solar System and wouldn't know the order of the planets if you asked him, but he'd got used to judging crimes superficially by their geographical size, and destroying the Solar system and possibly the known universe was, even to his limited imagination, a huge crime.

He regarded the scientist across the table with some satisfaction. The wretch looked a mess. His face was black and blue from beatings and his hands were shaking, but he was still conscious.

He put on a mock English accent.

"Well, I'm terribly sorry old chap for the mistreatment you've had. Really, I am," he grinned, "My men, you know, are usually well behaved, but we've never had a world-killer to deal with before."

The scientist spoke with some pain.

"It's going to be alright!"

"Nice try."

"How about my family?"

"What about them?"

“Where are they? How are they?”

“They were spirited away by some Rooter do-gooders in my army. It’s you we want.”

“I need to tell you. The crack will heal itself.”

“Those desk scribblers back in Washington, want you so you can be passed through a jury process, but they’re politicians, corrupt. They can have you, but after I’ve finished with you.”

The guard standing by the door looked a little uncertain at this. Fret seized his chance.

“What would root command say?”

The guard by the door dropped his rifle quite suddenly, which went off. A bullet hit the spartan white wall behind the general, who stood up, livid.

“Pinkus, you idiot. Get out!”

The guard picked up his rifle and ran out, sweating.

“Very clever. I can’t decide what else to do to you yet. So it’s back to solitary for you. Anticipation of pain is always most effective.”

“What do you want from me?”

“Fear. Do you know why people are freer after a war?”

“Er, no.”

“Because usually the public are so concerned to avoid their first kill and what that means about them being cosmically cursed, but when you've killed several real people in a war, one more makes no difference, and national rulers know that revolution is possible. That is why you as an innocent may not realise that I as an experienced soldier could snuff you out without any cosmic concern. Think on that."

As the scientist was led away, the general made sure the door had closed and then called his orderly in from the next room.

"Any news of his family?"

"No sir. They just disappeared, sir!"

"Damn portals – they're supposed to be banned."

"We can't fight physics, Sir."

"Maybe so, but you guys find them, or I'll have you all sent to the Middle east."

The day was not going well for the general. To top it all, his wife had just phoned him to announce that she'd become a Rooter, and she was going to have to 'divorce his military ass' to enter their weird concept of heaven. Luckily, he did not know that that was also, indirectly, Fret's fault.

Chapter 46

This is like the Stephen King novel 'Misery' thought Fret as he lay there on a gurney wallowing in pain, having been beaten up by just about every soldier that had felt like it, with the exception of a few, such as Pinkus, who had been Rooters and had refused. He missed Henryk, his son, as he lay there expecting the end. It was increasingly clear to him that he'd spent much of his life searching for new physics and too little of it paying attention to simpler things. He missed his son so much that when he looked at the wall, there was Henryk looking out of it.

"Dad, we found you!"

Fret was not in the clearest of frames of mind, so the significance of this event was lost on him.

"Hello Henryk," he said without enthusiasm and through swollen lips, believing it to be an illusion.

"Dad, we're going to get you out. Just wait for half an hour, Alright?"

"Alright, son."

Henryk disappeared and Fret burst into tears of frustration, desperation and loss. In extremis he'd always been susceptible to sudden bursts of irrational behaviour. He did not believe in the standard version of God, due partly to his desire for intellectual autonomy, but he did believe in a friendly spirit whose origin might, for example, be humans from the future reaching back through time to start their own development. This seemed to him to be, at least, rational, and probably more likely.

He was sure only that science did not answer everything and there was plenty of room for ideas beyond the logical. It was enough, and he now asked this mysterious God mechanism for help, an act of desperation. An echo came back from his own consciousness 'If a thing has value it'll be saved'.

He looked around with hope.

"Now would be a good time," he muttered under his breath.

Half an hour later he was still waiting.

"Well, thanks a lot."

The hallucination of his son had obviously failed to rematerialise.

Then in walked the guard.

"OK, physicist. Time for rough justice. This is for messing up my kids' future."

To Fret's horror he pulled out his gun.

A baseball bat appeared out of mid-air and waved around a while as the guard looked at it in dumb amazement. It then hit him sharply on the head and he crumpled in a heap on the floor.

"Dad!"

The excited face of Henryk appeared in mid-air.

“Fret!” It sounded like his wife.

“Fret, snap out of it and open your eyes!”

That was definitely his wife. He opened his eyes, now so swollen he could only see through a narrow slit. A portal was open, and in it stood his son, his wife, Chip and a man he didn’t know.

“Hey guys, are you real?”

“Yeah Dad. It’s us!”

“Am I glad to see yous! Especially you Henryk.”

“Shh,” they said.

“Dad, why is your face blue?”

“I got beaten up, a lot, but I think I can stand if someone can cut me loose.”

Chip and the unknown man jumped out of the portal which was about a metre above the floor and the newcomer gave a mock salute.

“I’m Enrico. I made contact with your family to help out. I’m an astrophysicist and I have some news, but we can talk later.”

“Well, thanks a lot, but can we hurry it up. I’m not especially fond of this place.”

“I can see why.”

Enrico started cutting away at the harness holding Fret down with his pen knife. Chip was just heading for the door to be a look-out when in walked a frowning Pinkus, rubbing his red hair. He saw his comrade on the floor and Fret being released. For a split second he looked at them all in surprise and then winked, smiled, put his thumbs up and quietly backed out of the door saying to the ceiling,

“For Root Command, I’d like Emily please...”

Chip turned to Fret, his face white.

“Thank God for Root Command.”

“Interesting statement!” said Fret.

When he was free, Fret turned to the portal to hug his son and was lifted and pushed through it by Chip and Enrico, into a large hall with a massive telescope in the centre.

“An observatory?”

“The Paranal Observatory in Chile. I work here.”

“Aren’t you impressed Dad? That I rescued you?” said Henryk.

“Yes, I think you’re absolutely amazing ... all of you, and I can’t thank you enough.”

With a wink, Enrico handed him a gun.

“Do you know how to use it?”

"No – I'm pretty inept that way."

"Bravo," said Gabriella.

Enrico decided to keep both guns, said,

"I have Mapuche ancestry. When survival is at stake you fight however you can. I should tell you of our history sometime."

Gabriella seemed to be on terms of friendly animosity with him.

"You're not the only race with painful history, you know?"

"Alright! Can I tell Fret the plan now?"

"Who's stopping you?"

"Here's the plan," said Enrico. "I guess you must have worked out that your portals create cylindrical horizons along the travel path and that they radiate due to Landauer's principle which makes them shrink."

"Yes! I know that, but the goons didn't believe me."

"I doubt they've read your papers, but I have, now. I loved your use of..."

Mum interrupted at this point, frustration boiling over…

"Look, congratulations can come later. Tell him the plan."

"Alright. As you know, we have a so-called crack that is freaking everyone out. We know it's going to disappear and everything will be OK, but no-one else does, and at this rate it'll take perhaps years to emit light and dissipate."

"Yes, we need to speed up the process, but how?"

"My younger brother is a Tin-Tin fan and I was watching the Castafiore Diamond with him the other day and in that story an opera singer breaks a glass with high pitched sound waves that resonate at just the right wavelength to break up the glass."

At this point, Gabriella returned with a chair for Fret and he collapsed onto it as if it was a water bed.

"I thought maybe we can break up the cylindrical horizon by treating it like a solid and firing sound waves down it."

"Of course," said Fret, jumping up and immediately falling down again. Chip caught him. After a pause Fret spoke.

"The sound waves will increase the surface area of the cylindrical horizon and increase the energy loss by Landauer's principle."

"Exactly. Not only that, but I contacted your friend at CERN, Prof Unz and he tested it on the horizon in your basement and it brightened but shrank significantly. It seems not much energy is required since the horizon thickness is something close to only 10^{-35} metres, the Planck length."

"The Planck length? Oh, thank God," said Fret, beaming despite the pain.

"Now we just need to stay alive long enough that the problem goes away."

Chapter 47

Enrico took Fret in his wheelchair, with Henryk, out onto the balcony for a cup of coffee.

"I'm afraid we can't do much about your injuries, the nearest doctor is a few hundred miles away, but I thought a cup of coffee would be welcome."

"Do you have tea? That's all I need."

"We have some bags of tea."

"Tea fixes everything. I'll make it."

The joy of talking to intelligent folk is that they understand things often just from context. It saves mouth-work.

"Understood. I wouldn't ask the English to make Cazuela."

After Fret had made some tea in the well-cleaned kitchen, with a little help with reaching the cupboards, they walked out onto the stainless steel balcony, a modern structure high up on the side of the building, and glanced up into the blue sky. The countryside around was as barren as a desert, probably because it was one, and the air was dry, making Fret's nose wrinkle. As Enrico explained to Henryk, it rarely rained and that was why the telescope had been built there. No clouds to block the view.

"Dad! Why can't we have blue sky like this in England?"

"Because the air we get blows off the Atlantic and there's too much moisture in it."

"So that's why we get clouds?"

"Yes. On the positive side, we have a lovely green landscape."

"And mud to play in!"

"And mud, yes."

Over to the west the sun was setting over the Pacific Ocean and it was hard for Fret to take in the relief at having escaped. An hour ago he'd assumed he was entering his last moments and fearing a painful death, and now, he was in this beautiful place with his family, and excitingly close to the largest telescope he'd seen in his life. He took a sip of tea, when it was offered and immediately his damaged lip exploded with pain and his howl of horror echoed over the dry, barren hills.

"You alright Dad?"

Dad was holding his mouth in his hands.

"Yes, I'm very happy to be here, son."

Enrico kept quiet, not wanting to interrupt the reunion, but he kept a close eye on the horizon for helicopters, knowing that, sooner or later the world would come barging in, like it always did.

They all, except Chip as lookout, went to sleep that night, feeling safe and when they awoke Fret felt a lot better, and made them all breakfast. The processes of natural repair had completed some of their work.

Prof Unz had been assaulting the crack with sound waves overnight – as expected very little sound was required to make a difference even to a horizon that stretched from the Earth to Mars since its edge was infinitesimally thin and so its volume was tiny[8] - and Gabriella had prepared some photos from the telescopes to prove that the Crack was shrinking and was ready to email it around the world.

The fact that it was shrinking was crucial because the vibration was making the crack emit far more Landauer light, which was doing nothing to reduce global concern.

"You realise, as soon as I email these photos all hell will break lose?" she said "Those who wish you ill, won't believe it and will come to try and discredit us, and the positive souls who might believe you will be powerless to act. So why don't you get away from here while you can?"

"But where? It's a desert in all directions! I'd rather stay here. Besides, they aren't going to attack an expensive observatory."

"We aren't going to put up much of a fight, so I do recommend you disappear in the desert. It'll give you

---

[8] The volume of the edge of the 'tunnel' to Mars = 2π x radius x edge thickness x distance to Mars at the time = 2π x 0.5 x 1.61×10^{-35} x 400×10^{9} m = 2×10^{-23} m^3. Small!

some time to think. Besides there's a valley that's beautiful out there, that we often camp in."

Henryk put his hand up, a habit he'd picked up at school.

"Dad. Let's not run away. Let's tell 'em how much fun it was!"

"I guess the bits you saw were fun."

"We did amazing things Dad. We stepped through the portal onto a beach. We rescued that man in London. We put an apple on Mars and we spoke to aliens."

"That's right. We did all of that."

"If they only knew, they'd love it, and want to do that too."

Enrico and Gabriella were rather puzzled by this.

"What guy in London. What Aliens?"

"See Dad? They don't even know. Tell them!"

"Yes, tell us," said Enrico seriously.

Gabriela grabbed Fret by the shoulders.

"Did you make contact with Root Command?"

"I suppose, in a manner of speaking."

"That's it. That's why Root Command contacted the Earth. We are now worthy, and it's all down to you."

Enrico was getting a little tired of Root Command, despite the fact that it had made possible his recent good fortune with Gabby. He had a more practical suggestion.

“That might be a good angle to get you out of this. I know someone who works for a TV company.”

“You want me on TV?” said Fret.

“Fret, darling,” said his wife, “you may have invented the portal, but let me tell you that when it comes to communication you haven’t a clue.”

“Who needs critics, when we have wives?” said Fret

She hit his arm playfully and then turned to Enrico.

“We’ll do it.”

Within an hour they had portaled off in various directions. Three hour later, ten US helicopters landed at the observatory to find no one there, and the only relevant thing they could find was a little note sellotaped to the largest telescope saying,

“We’ve gone into the desert.”

But despite several days search, snake bites, and a lot of cursing, the troops began to suspect they’d been had.

Chapter 48

Three scruffy people stood in what must have been one of the most spectacular rooms in the world. Through the window was a view over a darkening alpine valley, the lights of the village of Glarus scattered like stardust on the valley floor. They went out onto the balcony to see the immense peaks of the Alps rising dark blue and impossibly huge below the cerulean sky. The stars could be seen above the peaks and reminded Fret why he had built the portal,

"We can go there now, " he said to himself. A sense of confidence that he was on the right track returned.

Inside the room, the sofas, tables and carpet were russet, which thoughtfully brought out the warm colours in the cold scene outside. A huge roaring fire stood embedded in the right hand wall casting a brighter orange glow over everything. It was the sort of room that James Bond would have no problem seducing a Russian spy in, and as if this had been going on a few minutes ago before he jumped out of the window for a quick ski chase, a bottle of Champagne stood open in an ice bucket. Fret looked around for the woman Bond had left behind, no luck.

"Now this is more like it," said Mum. "When I first married you, I thought you'd be taking me to places like this, and now you are!"

"Hey. Stick with me baby."

A very famous TV presenter then walked through the door, immaculately clad, as they all seem to be, in suits and coloured tie. The four visitors started to feel distinctly underdressed. He spoke with a deep, rich voice that implied that the sound came from a voice box the size of Westminster Cathedral.

“Good evening. How do you like our interview room?”

Fret reply was less than appreciative.

“How can we have a serious interview with a view like that outside the window, Champagne in a bucket and a cosy fire?”

Mum gave him a nudge, but the celebrity was not to be deflected.

“We’ve found it puts people at ease. The mountains make them feel inconsequential and maybe more willing to open up, the fire makes them feel cosy and safe, and the Champagne, well, that has a more basic chemical effect.”

“It makes them feel wobbly?” said Henryk.

“Yes, Er... quite.” The presenter, more at home with interacting with Peers of the Realm than children, took a deep breath and asked.

“Alright Fret. Please sit on the left of the sofa, and I’ll sit at this end.”

At that moment, an aide came into the room, spoke quietly in the ear of the interviewer who looked at Fret wide eyed and said, very politely.

“I’m very sorry, but the interview has been cancelled.”

“Why?”

“Well…”

“I’m not surprised at all,” said Luther, stepping out of the fireplace.

The room was suddenly full of wide open mouths.

“Who the hell are ...?” said the aide, though halfway through saying it he tailed off as he realised exactly who it was.

“Jon Luther at your service,” said Luther and fired a stun dart at the celebrity and his aid who slowly collapsed onto the plush floor.

“It’s the only merciful thing to do to legacy media,” said Jon.

Fret was as surprised as everyone else.

“Well, it’s great to see you Jon, but why are you here?”

Several more men and women in yellow T-shirts were now walking out of the fireplace armed with stun guns. One of them said,

“Oh, diagonal alley!”, the others laughed.

Some took up places in the room and some dashed out into the corridor beyond.

“The corporations have decided not to allow you a show after all. They’ve realised what they have to lose with your portals - now they’ve been shown to be safe – everyone’s heard that the crack is dissipating, but governments are almost all saying it’s a hoax.”

“What do they have to lose?”

“Their security. How will they protect their possessions? Their luxury houses? Their bank vaults if everyone is suddenly allowed to zoom around the place at will, through walls and guards.”

“A change of plan then.”

“Yes, we’ll do it my way, but we’d better hurry up because there’s a crisis as Rooters spread – bad news for the corrupt - and they are undoubtedly rushing their armed forces over here to take you back into custody.”

At that moment a helicopter hove into view outside the window. It looked only superficially like a helicopter and more like a flying arsenal.

“Any questions?’ said Luther. “Get in the corridor!”

The helicopter opened fire.

Chapter 49

The window was shatter proof, and remained so for just long enough for everyone to pile out of the room, dragging the unconscious interviewer and his aid as well. They ended up in a tangled heap, panting heavily. The room then exploded as a tangled mess of tortured class.

“Is nowhere safe?” said Fret.

“That beautiful sofa! It’s now full of holes,” said Mum.

“That was awesome,” said Henryk.

Gunfire was now occurring all around them, and Luther explained that his people were forming a perimeter so that they could get to a broadcasting studio and start the broadcast, and indicated for them to follow him.

“I didn’t know you had people,'' said Fret.

“After you got me out I realised I needed a semi-military guard for my own safety, but we use only non-fatal weapons, stun guns that fire chemical darts.”

A very real bullet hit the ceiling not far from them.

“I wish my enemies would adopt a similar method,” he said.

He pointed to a door on the left with a sign outside it saying ‘Studio B’.

“Here we are – all the world is in there waiting to hear from you.”

They filed in, rather quickly and found a room rather less impressive than the russet one they had left and that had now been riddled with bullets.

“Is this it?” said Mum.

“It’s strictly utilitarian, this one, but it’ll work rather better.”

“Why?”

“Because you can’t be shot in it. Now sit down and we’ll get started, before they realise what’s happened and cut all the internet connections to the building.”

Half an hour later the hasty interview detailing the amazing things that had happened and how and why the Crack was safe and temporary, was uploaded onto bitchute and sent to the very few independent news-sites around the world.

“Now we just need a paper describing how you built the portal, so that anyone around the globe can make one. Here’s a laptop. Do you write in latex?”

“Yes, of course.”

“I thought you would. It’s installed. Now get writing.”

As if to emphasise the point a blast rocked the whole building. Henryk had now decided that the circumstances were veering from awesome to scary and was hugging his dad’s leg. Another explosion rocked the building and Luther’s laptop beeped at him.

"Damn, they've taken out the landline. We'll have to send it by mobile. How much of the paper have you written?"

"The title!"

"Hurry up! The future's at stake here."

"Look, I didn't invent this to save the future. I did it because I like creating things. I feel alive when I have my own ideas. I don't understand how it's all become so serious! Look at my son: he's scared! I'm a nervous wreck!"

"Welcome to the club," Luther giggled to himself.

"What's so funny?"

"Your life is just a wrecked as mine!"

"Yeah, great. The difference is, much of the world loved you. Only the powerful and their drones hated you. With me, everyone hates me!"

"That won't be true for long. You don't see what you've done yet, like I didn't."

"What have I done?"

"You've made a paradigm shift."

"I know that. Informational physics."

Luther grabbed Fret by the collar.

"Not only that: your discovery changes society as a whole. Don't you see? The whole idea of being rich is to hoard something like gold or money or something behind a wall. Your invention of a portal has made walls obsolete so the hoarders become normal again. It shakes up the hierarchy, until someone invents a portal blocker."

"I seem to remember the aliens said something similar."

"They may well be looking at our history with the benefit of hindsight. So, write that paper in a way everyone can understand, including the maths, and we'll send it everywhere. You've already shaken things up, and the video will help too. This'll be the final push. No science is complete without the rigorous maths, to make it predictive."

A full symphony was playing in John Luther's head, but it was suddenly interrupted by a penny whistle.

"No," said Fret.

"No?"

"I'm going to get my son to a place of safety first. I don't care about your revolution. Well, not enough to sacrifice my son."

"This is important, man!"

"Not to me. Help me save my son and I'll write it."

"I didn't want to tell you this, but I did not expect them to attack so soon. Our chances are not good."

"What do you mean? Chip'll get a portal through to us here won't he?"

"If he could've, he would've. They must have some problem shifting it from the fireplace to here."

"OK, we'll have to escape from here."

"We have about ten of my people here, but outside are most of the resources of the western nations. It's not to be sneezed at, you know? I can probably send a paper out from you, but I think we're personally in a bad way."

Henryk started to cry. His Mum had her head in her hands and was uncharacteristically silent.

Chapter 50

The zero-point field is everywhere, but people do not realise it. Like super-tankers in the Mediterranean we do not notice its waves, but they are there behind the scenes &, if you know how, they can work miracles.

Fret grabbed his son's head.

"We're going to get out of this, don't worry!"

"How Dad? That guy said we're doomed?"

"Oh, he's an Australian. Everything is upside down in Australia."

Henryk smiled.

"You mean like opposite day?"

"Exactly!"

"Great, Dad. What's the plan?"

Luther was mumbling to himself over his laptop. Maybe I can still get a signal through. Yes, there's a residual...'

A lightbulb switched on in Fret's head.

"What did you say?"

"What? Well, I might be able to access the internet through a wire that still connected, a residual signal, you know?"

"That's it! We know that slices through space leave a residual. That is what caused the Crack."

"So?" said Luther.

"The portal you came out of should have left a residual. All we have to do is catch and retune it."

"And how do we do that?"

"It's an area of low intensity zero-point field waves, like the channels that Henryk & I make in the sand. All we have to do is make sure it's deep at this end and the water will flow here. We need to set up an array of semi-conductors in just the right shape, and the end of the portal, the old tunnel, if you like, will latch onto it like a fish on a line."

Luther sat back and folded his arms.

"That's great, where are we going to get conductors from at a time like this? And don't they have to be in exactly the right position? I remember you had to use a laser to position them before."

"It will be much easier to catch a residual."

"OK, then."

"I'll need your laptop."

"What for?" said Luther rather possessively.

"It's got semi-conductors in it."

"You keep your hands off my laptop, it's our only possible way to get a message out."

"Get a message out and we ourselves won't get out."

“You really think this’ll work?”

“Yes!”

Gun fire sounded outside and one of Luther’s team, a martial-arts type with muscles, ran into the room.

“We can’t hold them for long. They’re using drones. A portal would be good.”

Luther tossed his laptop to Fret.

“Go on and do it, but hurry.”

With that he pulled out his stun gun, and went out of the room and Fret began to disassemble the laptop.

Chapter 51

Chip was close to tears. The portal had failed and the reason wasn't clear.

"Goddamned thing!"

He'd rebooted the computer, he was more familiar with computers than actual physical objects, but he suspected that they had not closed the portal in time to avoid shrapnel from Switzerland. That had damaged a tile.

Brus banged into the room carrying a lot of laser equipment.

"Ve vill haff to measure whole thing again," he said.

"That'll take hours."

"Vhat is alternative?"

Chip raised his arms in despair and they started setting up the laser equipment. A TV in the corner of the room was showing the stand-off in Switzerland as it burbled on in praise of the International Coalition who were heroically fighting to destroy the scientist-turned-galactic-terrorist and the dangerous subversive Jon Luther holed up in the building.

Gabriella was pacing up and down.

"Root command will provide, if we do the right thing."

"Great! What's that?"

As they were waiting for Gabriella to state her latest epistle, there was indeed a voice, carried as if on the wind.

"Did you hear that?" said Chip.

"No, what is it?"

"Could have sworn I heard a voice."

They all listened intently as the tiniest of whispers came to them, amid static.

"M ### Ely ### Up ### 1mm!"

"Did you hear that?"

"Root command is trying to get though!"

"OK, but what did it say?"

"Please repeat!" Chip shouted at the metamaterial array.

"Moo ### E ### three up one ### mili ###"

Slowly, and with a bizarre mix of colours and rainbows a piece of paper slowly appeared out of thin air, as if printed by the vacuum itself, and drifted down to the floor. It said on it,

"Move element 3 up 1.2 mm"

Chip and Brus looked at each other in some puzzlement.

"Which one is element 3?" said Brus.

“How should I know?”

Gabriella, convinced this was Root Command and thinking of Christmas said,

“Let’s send a message back to Santa.”

Brus nodded.

“Sounds good to me!”

So they wrote on the back ‘Which is element 3?’ rolled it up and held it up at the point it had appeared. It disappeared. A minute passed and then the rolled up piece of paper was thrown back.

“Top = one, count clockwise. Quick!”

They found the element of the array, Brus held a metre ruler next to it anchored on the floor and Chip pushed it up by very roughly 1 mm. Immediately a wind rushed into the portal as the atmospheric pressure equalised itself between where they were and the high altitude in Switzerland, and then Henryk came through, then his mother, who was not in a good mood and once she’d brushed herself off, said.

“Well done, you got it fixed.”

“Yes. Thanks for the messages you guys sent through.”

“What messages?”

“I told you,” said Gabriella, “Root Command!”

“Madre de Dios,” said Enrico.

Unfortunately, Enrico waved his arm a little too wide and one of the elements of the portal was bent out of shape. The portal closed with Fret, Jon and his team left behind.

Chapter 52

As Heisenberg found, the uncertainty of time of a quantum system (denoted as Δt) multiplied by the uncertainty in its energy (denoted as ΔE) must be above the constant number $\hbar/2$ ($\Delta t \Delta E \sim \hbar/2$), so if one could somehow reduce the uncertainty in energy, what would happen to time? This, of course, no-one knows. Well, almost no-one.

How can you really measure time? Of course, you can't measure it directly, that was one of Einstein's contributions to human progress. We always measure time by looking at the progress of mechanical or electromagnetic processes. We call them clocks. Let us imagine a clock formed by light bouncing between two mirrors. Each bounce on a mirror is a tick. The light must travel mirror-mirror at the speed of light. Otherwise, as Einstein reasoned, light's speed would have been measured differently in different parts of the spinning world and it had not been.

Now imagine you move the clock to the side: the light has to follow the movement, as well as move up and down to form the clock. So it has further to go and the clock slows, as we said above, light speed cannot vary, even in relative motion. You might think this is just a superficial slowing, but Einstein was a follower of Mach who said, to put it crudely "Reality is what we <u>can</u> see" so if you see the clock slowing then we can only assume that that is time. What other measure do we have of time? None. All concepts, said Mach, must be linked to direct observables, and so we must say time itself slows upon relative movement.

Heisenberg's formula implies that if we reduce the amount of energy in the vacuum, ΔE, as Fret was now attempting, then Δt[9] will increase. This can be done by a horizon which damps the quantum energy field, or, say, by using high frequency electromagnetic waves. Either way, time will dilate. What would that look like?

From General Naille's point of view, he had just strode through the door like the bold man he was, amid innocent sheep, but from the point of view of Fret and Luther the image of him was time-dilated and smeared out into the many possible pathways he had available to him. It looked as if someone had taken a long exposure photograph. Fret was tapping frantically on a laptop.

A couple of antennas had been placed next to the laptop. These antennas were not capable of projecting a horizon themselves but using high frequency electromagnetic waves they were damping the quantum vacuum there (decreasing ΔE). This was causing dilated or 'fuzzy time' (increased Δt). If time is more uncertain, this means that you are able to see both the future and the past together so all processes become smeared out, as was happening to the biological process called Naille. From Fret and Luther's point of view, they could see the cloud of possibilities of what General Naille would do in the future. Naille, being the process, could not.

---

[9] In our universe this pathway is being opened up by papers such as McCulloch & Gine, 2021. The EPR paradox & the uncertainty principle. Modern Phys. Lett. B, 35, 4, 2150072.

As Fret adjusted the emissions of the antennae the possibility of a bullet slowly moved from Naille's gun towards Luther but it was insubstantial, like a ghost, passed through Luther with no harmful effect and with another adjustment from Fret it retreated slowly back into the gun.

"Stand somewhere else," said Fret.

"Absolutely!" said Luther and stepped aside.

"We can see his future, but he can't," said Fret.

"Handy," said Luther.

Luther caught on quick, and took direct action, leapt forward into the cloud of the General's possibilities, avoiding any of the potential bullets emanating from him, and hit him randomly but non-lethally in several places with a plank of wood from the shattered door. Naille collapsed, unconscious, and so did his possibilities, a deletion of information that omitted a little of Landauer's quantum heat.

"You're certainly full of surprises," said Luther.

"I always wanted to try that," said Fret, trying to appear calm, but his voice wavered a little from shock.

As if by magic, a portal appeared. Henryk was looking out of it.

"Jump through Dad. We're rescuing you, again!"

"Are we invited too?" said Jon, a little sarcastically.

Jon called his remaining troops back and after a little rear-guard action, Fret grabbed his laptop and shouted at Naille, who was now groaning on the floor,

"We let you live. Remember that!"

"What was that?" said Jon.

"Just concluding an argument we had earlier,"

and they all jumped through the portal, to safety.

Chapter 53

The Executors of Root Command loved Fret's new physics. Finally scientists were getting to grips with the sub-material and digital nature of reality, a nature that they were used to, having grown up with video games.

Of course, this was only the latest example of humans understanding the cosmos through an analogy with their latest technology, but although it is never the final word, it was at least more hopeful than the doom-laden machine-inspired cosmos of Newton. The cosmos is not a machine running down, but a game growing up. The whole paradigm, as well as being new science, also quickly solidified into a religion, or maybe more a way of life, but a moral one since it pointed out, as most good religions do, that a person should be judged not by accidents of birth but by their actions in the world, just as they are judged in video games and elevated to the next level or not.

There were still competitive people, of course, probably more so than before given that they knew they were in a game being judged by Root Command, but instead of showing their abilities through expensive cars or the number of digits in their bank statements, they strived to create substantial things or ideas that contributed to good, and by which they might be promoted by Root Command to the next level. It was not your Grandma's idea of heaven but it was effective and in the here and now, and slowly chaos turned into the beginnings of a golden age.

Freed from the bounds of Earth by the portal, people went to the Moon and Mars, and even, some of them, to Proxima Centauri, Tau Ceti and further afield. There they set up weird and wild communities, some of them boldly capitalist, some based on The Book of Mormon, and some based on a complete clothing-ban. One adopted the original series of Star Trek as a model. All of them were creative and new. Even the Amish took to the portal and colonised many of these planets. Evolution in its wisdom would decide which social systems would prevail and spread the fastest.

The only minor problem, to Fret, was, where was the previous wave of humanity? If they had indeed existed and had portals, where had they gone? Had something nasty come out of their portals, or, by now, had they simply escaped, as Douglas Adams might have said, at right angles to reality?

Chapter 54

It was a long time before they returned home. Their street was immaculately tidy, with flowers everywhere, and there seemed to be a lot of prams parked by the doors. The house was full of the debris left by rampaging American troops, cigarette stubs and some graffiti. Mum got organised with a redecoration – another dream come true – and a portal disrupter, a new invention rapidly spreading, was set up to stop people from beaming in.

One day in spring, as the red roses were blooming by the front door they all met up at the refurbished house. Fret put his rucksack down in the hall as he always had, and made for the spanking new kitchen to put the kettle and the radio on. A brilliant song by the Beatles blasted out.

"I don't remember this one," said Fret.

The radio announced quite casually.

"This was Golden Age from the Beatles, released when they reformed in 1971 on their All Things Pass LP."

They all looked at each other gleefully.

"Next level up," they said.

Chip was disappointed.

"We save the world, and all we get is a new Beatles song?"

"There'll be more changes, I'm sure," said Fret.

"Eesh. What bothers me, " said Chip, "is whether this has been going on all the time, or has it just started now?"

"You've just given the philosophers a happy couple of centuries of debate with that one," said Fret.

Gabriella ambled slowly in her very pregnant state down to the basement. A few minutes later, armed with tea, they followed to find her before the portal taking photos.

"You, alright?" said Enrico.

"Yes. It's just that this is the portal through which Root Command called us. It should be a shrine."

"Good idea! We can sell tickets to see it," said Chip, earning a frown from Gabriella and a wink from Enrico.

Brus with a cup of black tea was loving every minute. He grabbed both Chip and Enrico round the shoulders.

"Guys, maybe Mericans not so bad. I have MBA. Let's talk business."

"Hey," said Chip with mock anger, "Don't go Russian into things," to a puzzled look from Brus.

Ignoring Brus, and bristling at being called an American, Enrico broached the subject of the pattern he had seen in The Crack, and recorded as well. Gabriella nodded enthusiastically.

"We need to understand it – it might be a message from Root Command."

“We will,” said Enrico, “Although whatever Root Command is, I suspect it’s way higher than we can imagine.”

Dad was fingering the pieces of the portal, remembering how many years of effort had gone into conceiving and building it.

“Well, Henryk. Glad to be back?”

“I love seeing my Lego again. Can we build something?”

“Sure. I’ll play as long as you want. What shall we build?”

“I’m tired of portals. How about a disrupter? They’re cool.”

“No problem.”

At that moment the house phone rang and Mum answered it,

“That’s Oxford University. They want a word!”

Fret instinctively leaped at the phone, Henryk looked downcast, but just before he got to the phone, Fret stopped.

“You know what? Let them wait. We’ve got some playing to do.”

His wife looked on as they played. Her husband had always played with Henryk and had fun, but something had changed. He seemed to be more appreciative of the present. He'd turned the world upside down, sure, but maybe he'd also turned himself the right way up.

**** THE END ****

Printed in Great Britain
by Amazon

29658110R00109